Challenge of the Void!

The Head signed off with the Service toast, ''Here's to tomorrow, fellows and friends. May we all live to see it!'' He acted as if this were just an ordinary assignment, even though no case the d'Alemberts worked on could be called ordinary.

But this one was special, and they all knew it. For the first time they would be walking into a trap designed specifically for them. They would need courage, strength, and not a little luck to escape this particular menace.

ECLIPSING BINARIES
E.E. "DOC" SMITH

WITH STEPHEN GOLDIN

BERKLEY BOOKS, NEW YORK

ECLIPSING BINARIES

A Berkley Book / published by arrangement with
the author

PRINTING HISTORY

Berkley edition / March 1983

ISBN: 0-425-05848-4

A BERKLEY BOOK ® TM 757,375
The name ''BERKLEY'' and the stylized ''B'' with design
are trademarks belonging to Berkley Publishing Corporation.

PRINTED IN THE UNITED STATES OF AMERICA

1
The War Against SOTE

Being summoned to Lady A's office was never a casual matter. Tanya Boros had to pass an ID and weapons checkpoint before she was even allowed into the elevator tube taking her down to the lowest basement level. There she passed a human-supervised retinascope check and a weapons detector scan. Then she had to walk alone down a brightly lit L-shaped corridor with camera eyes watching her every step of the way. The walls were gray and completely bare except for the innocuous-looking small projections she assumed were blaster barrels pointed directly at her.

As she turned right at the far end of the hallway, she came abruptly to the heavy gray magnisteel door that was the final barrier to Lady A's office. There were some people—ones who had made serious mistakes on their assignments—who had gone through this door and never been seen alive again, though admittedly such cases were rare. Lady A normally dealt with faulty subordinates in a more efficient manner, letting others on her staff do the dirty work. More often a visit to Lady A meant a tongue-lashing for some slipup, some operation that had gone less smoothly than planned even if it was ultimately successful. Most of Lady A's plans did go smoothly, but she was a perfectionist and did not tolerate even minor faults in her hirelings.

Even at best, being called to this office merely meant another hard, demanding job from a taskmaster who was never satisfied. There was still much to do if the conspiracy was to topple the Stanley dynasty from the Imperial Throne, and Lady A could never quite understand why her inferiors did not measure up to her own impeccable standards.

For all these reasons, Tanya Boros was understandably nervous as she stood before the ponderous gray door. As far as she *knew* she'd done nothing wrong—but innocence was not always an alibi in Lady A's court. The woman who ran this vast, galaxy-wide conspiracy had been in a foul mood for the last six months, ever since the failure of Operation Annihilate. All plans had been put into abeyance while the conspiracy was evaluated from top to bottom and its goals reassessed. Things were now starting to move again—but Tanya Boros didn't know what place she would fill in the new organization, and that bothered her.

Nervously she inserted her comparison disc into the appropriate slot and put her eyes to the viewer so the retinascope could check her pattern. Even after all the previous precautions, no one was permitted into Lady A's office without undergoing one final identity check; Lady A was too thorough for anyone to catch her unawares.

Boros's retinal patterns matched the ones on her identity card, which the door returned to her. Then the heavy security portal swung slowly outward and Lady A said,

"Come in, Tanya. I've been expecting you." Tanya Boros obeyed.

The office was quite dim after the bright lighting of the corridor outside. Three of the walls were covered with cream-colored raw silk but were otherwise bare of adornment. The fourth wall, opposite the door, was one large triscreen bearing the image of a mist-shrouded stream tumbling between ancient eroding mountains.

The floor was hard and black, polished smooth as ice; it was difficult to walk on it without making noise, and impossible to move quickly without slipping. Two black lacquered chairs—neither very comfortable—and a black lacquered table between them were the only concessions to a visitor's comfort.

At the far end of the room near the left-hand corner stood a large, glowing green egg. Carved from solid jade, it pulsated slightly from internal illumination. As the egg pivoted slowly, Boros could see a computer terminal and keyboard built into the interior, which had been hollowed out to form a comfortable seat. The computer terminal, it was rumored, allowed instant access to all the conspiracy's files as well as a direct telecom link to the mysterious person known only as C. That immense jade egg represented the very heart of the conspiracy—and seated within this egg, back straight and looking as though she'd been born to rule the universe, was Lady A.

The woman who ran the greatest conspiracy in human history was of average height—but that was the only thing average about her. Tanya Boros, never modest and renowned for her own attractiveness, always felt plain in the presence of this magnificent woman. Her figure and face were of classic beauty, mature but unwrinkled, and there was something inhumanly cold about them. She wore a tight-fitting dress of jade green silk one shade darker than the egg about her, with gold and silver phoenixes embroidered on the shoulders and sleeves. Her jet black hair, tightly braided, was draped casually across her left shoulder, and her green eyes peered out from beneath those arching black brows with painful intensity.

As the door closed behind her, Tanya Boros stood in this regal presence not knowing what to say. Even though she'd been raised in the upper echelons of galactic nobility, she'd never met anyone else who was as awe-inspiring as Lady A.

"Don't just stand there, child," Lady A said. "Have a seat." She gestured with a perfectly manicured hand at one of the two black lacquered chairs.

"Thank you," Boros said, taking the indicated seat. The two women sat in silence for a long moment. Boros grew increasingly uncomfortable at the appraising scrutiny she was being given. It felt as though Lady A were weighing her very soul and finding it a feather's weight this side of perfection.

"We haven't had much chance to talk recently, have we?" Lady A said at last, breaking the unbearable silence.

"No, ma'am."

"Not since Gastonia, really."

Boros's eyes widened a little. "That really wasn't my fault. I did everything expected of me. ... ."

Lady A raised a hand to silence her. "No one's blaming you for anything. Don't start looking for excuses where none are due; it's bad form. No, everything on Gastonia itself went as scheduled. You performed admirably. The reason for failure lay elsewhere."

She settled back in the glowing egg, but her body never fully relaxed. "To be candid, I suppose I should admit the fault was mine."

"Oh no," Boros said quickly. "It was purely accidental . . ."

"No." Lady A slammed her left fist on the side of the

egg with a force that echoed through the quiet room. "If I won't accept that excuse from my inferiors, I have no right to lean on it myself. There are no accidents; there's only sloppy planning or inadequate execution."

Unexpectedly she stood up and walked a few paces from her egg, staring out at the triscreen with her back to Boros. "We've spent the last six months analyzing the failure, both from our side and from the reports we've seen in the Empire's records. If I needed an excuse, I could blame it on that robot who's now so conveniently destroyed, for its failure to make certain Commander Fortier was dead before proceeding with its plans. That was the pivotal factor.

"But to be honest, I must look beyond that to the errors in planning that made such a mistake not only possible, but fatal to our plans. The fact is, the operation was overplanned. In trying to be so clever, we outfoxed ourselves. We had the force and the resources to make the attack work. If we'd just gone ahead and bulled our way through, it *would* have worked. Instead, we tried too hard for finesse, and it threw us just enough off balance to let the Imperial forces recover. We lost a great deal in that disaster, more than just the seventy-five percent of our fleet. But it's a mistake that will not happen again—I swear it by the throne I intend to take."

Tanya Boros felt distinctly uneasy. Lady A was not known for being particularly introspective, or for admitting weaknesses or imperfections in front of her subordinates. Why was she behaving so uncharacteristically in front of Boros? What had caused her to reveal this unexpected side of her nature?

The mask of perfection was suddenly back in place as though it had never been awry. Lady A turned abruptly away from the triscreen and returned to the jade egg to face Boros.

"All this, of course," she said, "is of only peripheral

interest to you. You need not concern yourself, at present, with matters of policy. That will come later, if you develop as well as I hope. In the meantime, I have to know whether you are prepared to begin assuming responsibility for your proper role in this conspiracy.''

"My proper role?'' Boros was puzzled. "I don't understand. I've always taken your orders, since you first contacted me on Gastonia. I didn't like being forced to stay there, but, as you said, it was out of the way and no one noticed me. What do you consider my 'proper role' to be?''

Lady A gave her a long, frowning stare. "Have you forgotten your heritage this easily—you, the only child of Emperor Stanley Nine's oldest son? You have a better claim to the throne than the silly little snip who sits there now!''

A trace of Boros's old haughtiness returned. Straightening her back, she said, "Of course I haven't forgotten. But it didn't seem to matter to anyone else.''

"It matters to me,'' Lady A said with conviction. "This revolution is dedicated to restoring the proper order of things.''

"Am I to be made Empress, then?'' No matter how sincere the woman's voice was, Boros could not bring herself to believe Lady A was going to all this trouble purely for her benefit.

A tiny hint of a smile touched the corners of Lady A's lips. "Well, perhaps not yet. I *was* reserving that for myself. But you will receive a position commensurate with your heritage. I have special plans for you, my dear, that you can't even begin to guess.''

"And what does C say to all this?''

The smile broadened on Lady A's face. "To show you how much I trust you, I'll let you in on the best-kept secret in the Galaxy: There is no one named C. He is purely a myth created to confuse our enemies into thinking the conspiracy is more complex than it really is. All orders from C are *my* orders relayed through a special switchboard to appear as though they're coming from elsewhere. No such human being exists. You're now only the second person in the universe to know that.''

Again Boros felt uneasiness creep over her. Lady A was being far too open, and that was suspicious. ''Why are you telling me all this?'' she asked.

Lady A's mood shifted instantly to anger. ''I open my heart to you and receive distrust.'' She stood again, and in three long strides she was before Boros's chair. Lifting the younger woman effortlessly by the front of her tunic collar, Lady A held her a few centimeters off the ground and said with crystalline enunciation, ''You now have two choices, my dear. You either pledge me your unswerving, undivided loyalty and love, or I'll crush your skull until your brains trickle down your neck. You do not leave this room alive until I am assured the information you have is safe. You betrayed your father with a few inadvertent words; I'll not have you do the same to me. Do I make myself clear?''

For a long moment, Tanya Boros was too frightened to say anything. She knew her life was dangling by a very slender thread, and the wrong word—or even the right word with the wrong inflection—would give that thread a sudden snap. She considered her next words very carefully.

''Yes, ma'am,'' she said slowly. ''I am completely loyal to you. No one can doubt that. I've obeyed you completely from the first moment I met you on Gastonia. It's just . . . I didn't expect . . . I . . . I was surprised . . . I'm sorry. It won't happen again.''

Another eternity passed as those intense green eyes pierced all the way to her soul. Then slowly Lady A lowered the younger woman to the floor and loosened her grip on the front of the tunic. Boros was shaken. She had not known her superior was that strong. Even now, looking at the other woman's slender frame, she found it difficult to believe.

"You must never question me or my motives again," Lady A said in calm tones as she resumed her place in the glowing egg. "I have reasons for everything I do and say. It's not your place to understand them, merely to obey commands. If you do, you'll be richer for it; if you don't, you'll be dead. That should be reason enough."

"Yes, Gospozha."

The traces of a smile returned to Lady A's lips. "That's much better. Always respect your elders, child. Now that I've made my point, I will explain some of my thinking—not because you asked, but because I think it's better if you know something of what's going on.

"As I was saying, the failure of Operation Annihilate hurt our cause badly. We are not strong enough to make another frontal attack on the Empire for quite some time. We're far from defeat—the Empire still does not realize how thoroughly we have infiltrated and undermined their structure—but we'll have to return to more guerilla-style tactics for a while.

"What we need primarily is time to build up our strength again. We were able to do that the first time because SOTE spent so much time chasing your father we could work in virtual obscurity. Given those conditions, we could rebuild our forces in just a short while.

"Unfortunately, we no longer have such an effective smokescreen. The Service of the Empire now knows we exist, and they won't stand idly by and let us re-arm ourselves. We have the power to cause such chaos that SOTE would be too busy fighting a thousand different small fires to pay much attention to us—but that would tip our hand prematurely. That is something we will not do;

we must preserve a few secrets until the final confrontation is assured.

"Therefore we must declare war on SOTE itself. So far the Service has been but an annoying pest, but it distracted us just enough from our true goal that we miscalculated. The time has come to rid ourselves of the peskier elements within that organization. You will play a key part in that campaign. We have a command post called Battlestation G-6. . . ."

"That's one of the automated ones, isn't it?" Boros blurted.

Lady A stopped and looked hard at the younger woman. "I can see," she said after a moment, "that our internal security needs tightening. That was *supposed* to be secret. Don't worry, the fault is not yours," she added as Boros began to quiver again. "You can't help what you over-hear. It's the people who did the *talking* who are in trouble." Her fingers moved quickly over the keyboard in the side of the egg as she entered into the computer a reminder to deal with the problem.

"But returning to your question, yes, G-6 is almost entirely automated. You will be the only person aboard. I want a live person there to supervise the activities."

To say that Tanya Boros was disappointed with her assignment would have been a vast understatement. She was a social creature who liked to have other people around her—particularly men. Even among Earth's deca-dent elite, she had been notorious as one of the more promiscuous members. Gastonia had been a hardship for her. Even though Lady A had arranged for her to stay at the command house rather than in the village with the other condemned traitors—and Boros still could not under-stand why she'd been so favored—there had been no men except the guards, and they were an unimaginative group at best. Occasionally she had kidnapped men from the village for her pleasure. Of course, since only a few people in the village were allowed to know about the house's existence, she couldn't let the kidnapped men return, and had been forced to have them killed after a while. Still, Gastonia had provided her with *some* of life's simple pleasures.

But now she was being sent to an automated battlestation, with no companionship except robots and computers. It seemed she was merely trading one exile for another.

She was quite careful, though, not to let her disappointment show on her face. She'd already experienced Lady A's anger once, and she wasn't about to risk it a second time. She merely said, in as neutral a voice as she could muster, "What's my assignment?"

"Your orders will be waiting for you there when you arrive; that way, if anything should happen to you en route you can't give away the plan. You'll travel in a special ship that will allow you to dock with the battlestation. That is the *only* ship the station will allow to approach it; any others will be before they can get close. The station can defend itself automatically; you'll be perfectly safe once you get there."

Tanya Boros left Lady A's office feeling scarcely better than when she'd entered.

Weeks later, many parsecs away on the planet Arcta in Sector Twenty-Nine, a call came into SOTE's planetary headquarters. Its priority coding was Class Six, "critical," so it received instant attention from Colonel Patrick Hein, the officer in charge. Even if it had been coded as Class One, however, Hein would have paid attention—for the call came from two agents who identified themselves only as Wombat and Periwinkle.

Those two codenames commanded instant respect within the Service of the Empire, for it was known they were the organization's best undercover agents. Only a handful of people in the upper echelons knew their true identities, but everyone in the Service knew those two agents were to be obeyed. Their investigations·were key to the security of the Empire, and they had to have utmost cooperation at the local levels if they were to be efficient.

The call came in via an official Service scrambler, so Hein got on the vidicom and spoke directly. "What can I do for you?" he asked.

There was no visual image coming from the sender, but that was only to be expected; these agents would want to keep their identities hidden. "How many people do you have here on Arcta?" a man's voice asked.

"There are nine currently available, myself included."

"I'm not talking about 'currently available.' I mean total, if you pull everyone off current duty for a special assignment. How many?"

Hein barely hesitated. "Fourteen, but some of them are on pretty important missions . . ."

"That might just be enough. Periwinkle and I have pretty important missions, too. We'll need everyone you've got. We've got a gang of traitors trapped in their hideout, but we'll need help prying them out." He gave the location and continued, "Can you get all your people there within three hours?"

"If you want them, you've got them." Pulling some of his people out of their present assignments was a big sacrifice and months of work would be lost—but assisting Wombat and Periwinkle always took top priority. By helping them he could hope to win some good words in the official report of their mission.

Without further word of explanation, Agent Wombat cut the circuit. Colonel Hein didn't consider it rude; agents in the field didn't always have time for the niceties. Within a few minutes he was arranging calls to all his own agents, giving them the rendezvous coordinates. Once that was done, he had to arrange for weapons and transportation. Wombat hadn't told him how large a mob he'd be facing, so he picked armament with maximum firepower and versatility.

The last thing he did before leaving his office was to enter a record of the call in his official daily report. This sounded like a dangerous job; if he didn't come back, there had to be some record so Headquarters on Tellus would know what had been going on.

Arcta was a cold world, circling its red dwarf star near the outer limits of the zone of habitability. Its north polar ice cap was a barren stretch of glacial ridges and valleys, almost totally uninhabited. Here, in the midst of a howling gale, was the spot where Wombat had asked to rendezvous— on the top of a bluff overlooking a narrow valley carved out by a river that was currently frozen. By the side of the frozen river was a two-story prefab building, presumably the hideout Wombat had mentioned.

Hein and his agents were gathered on the bluff within the time allotted. It hadn't been easy, and some of the agents had been forced to come here ill-prepared for the freezing weather. Most of them sat in their copters with the heaters on, awaiting further instructions. Hein looked around for some sign of the two agents who'd summoned them all here.

A copter appeared hovering overhead and the vidicom in Hein's vehicle came to life. "Have you got them all?" the voice of Wombat asked.

"All present and accounted for," Hein said proudly.

"Good. The gang we're after is holed up in there, as you may have guessed. There are somewhere between fifteen and twenty of them—a bit too many for us to tackle ourselves. We want your people to go in and get them.

Take as many alive as possible—we hope to get some good information out of them.''

"What about you?" Hein asked.

"Periwinkle and I have decided it's best not to show our faces just yet. We'll hover up here and keep the area covered in case any of them escape and get past you.''

"Smooth," the colonel nodded. He looked over the valley with a practiced eye and then gave the deployment order to his shivering troops. Within minutes, the team from SOTE had moved out and down the sides of the bluff in an attack on the criminal headquarters.

Going down the face of the bluff was the most dangerous part of the assault, for the agents were easy targets against the cliff. They drew no enemy fire, however, and Hein prayed his luck would continue. Maybe the enemy had no long-range weapons, or maybe they just wanted to save themselves for the closer battle. In any case, he knew his agents were trained and ready to cope.

When the entire assault team was down on the valley floor, they started moving across the white, lightly packed snow toward the building. They crept in, bending low and taking advantage of any natural cover this sparse landscape presented. Still there was no enemy fire. That could be a good or a bad sign, and Hein was becoming nervous. As a good commander, he had to assume the worst.

"Are you sure they're in there?" he asked over his portable comlink to the copter hovering above.

"They're there, all right," Wombat said. "They're trying to lull you into a false sense of security. Don't be fooled.''

Slowly Hein and his team closed in on the quiet building, blasters at the ready to return enemy fire that never came. At last they were right up against the walls, stationed on either side of the doors and windows of the first floor. At a silent signal from Hein, they burst through the openings, steeled to meet tough resistance.

The ground floor of the building was deserted.

Perplexed, Hein pointed for some of his agents to go upstairs while he returned to the comlink. "The place seems empty," he reported.

"Are all your people in there? Have they checked everywhere?"

"That's what they're doing right now."

A single blaster beam from the waiting copter lashed downward, striking a bundle of explosives planted on the roof.

With a ground-shattering roar that touched off avalanches seven kilometers away, the building exploded in a blinding flash of light. Dust and debris were thrown high into the air, only to fall again like a blanket of new snow upon the ruins of what had once been a building.

The copter circled for several minutes over this scene of desolation, checking to make sure there was not the slightest sign of life in the wreckage. Once convinced, the craft and its passengers flew off, content with their day's work.

2
Deadly Doubles

The small spaceship approached the asteroid belt at great speed. The space debris ahead was not so densely packed that it was an impassable hazard, but it did serve as a natural obstacle course to be successfully astrogated. A wrong move could be fatal. It would take fast reflexes and steady nerves to make it through without mishap.

In the co-pilot's seat, Jules d'Alembert asked, "Are you sure you're ready for this?"

The pilot, his brother-in-law, took a deep breath and let it out slowly. "If I don't do it now, I never will," Pias Bavol said. "I've gone through here at cruising speed, but I'll have to do better than that. Lady A won't let me cruise along casually if she gets me in her sights."

"_Eh, bien,_" Jules said. "The show's all yours."

Pias stretched his fingers and swiveled his shoulders a few times to limber them up, then leaned forward to concentrate on the control screen. The panel extended before him, a broad expanse covered with buttons, knobs,

switches, screens, dials, gauges, and glowing lights. Pias
extended the protective screens to their limits to shield the
ship from a stream of particles too small to be detected on
the sensors. He cut off the rear scanners and focused all
the vessel's detection capacity to a rapid forward scan. He
wasn't worried about asteroids overtaking him from the
rear—but the defensive shields would be useless against a
flying piece of rock more than a couple of meters in
diameter.

After one last millisecond of hesitation, he turned off the
automatic pilot and took complete manual control of the
spacecraft. The autopilot would have been useful for dodging one rock at a time, at slow speeds, but it tended to
overcompensate; in swerving to avoid one oncoming asteroid it could very well steer them directly into another and
not be able to correct in time. Fine tuning like that was
still the province of human reflexes.

Reflexes were one of Pias's greatest assets. Both he and
Jules were natives of planets whose gravity was three
times stronger than that of Earth. Over the generations,
nature had bred their ancestors for lightning reactions.
Pias, Jules, and all their kin could move at speeds that
dazzled people from normal gravity worlds.

The first obstacles were starting to appear on the scanners now, along with computer-generated arcs showing
their orbits relative to the ship. No danger so far; the
closest would miss by more than a kilometer. Pias had
arbitrarily set himself a safety range of two hundred meters. Anything closer than that would be avoided; beyond
that limit, he refused to worry about it.

In the seat beside him, he knew Jules was watching the
screen as intently as he was. At the slightest hint that Pias
might not be able to handle the situation, Jules was prepared to switch control over to his co-pilot's board and get
them out of trouble. It was comforting, in a way, to have

such a backup, because Pias knew Jules was an expert pilot. All the same, he was hoping it wouldn't be necessary.

More obstacles were appearing on the scanner now, ranging in size from small boulders to large mountains. Pias ignored the size and mass data also displayed on the screen; all he cared about was how close the object's path would come to his ship's.

The first indication of something that would come within the safety limits appeared. Even though the computer said it would miss the ship by a good seventy-five meters, Pias wanted to take no chances at this stage. His hand moved to the attitude controls and made ever so minor a course correction; they flew past the rock without trouble.

They were starting to reach the thickest part of the belt. The asteroid zone within the DesPlainian solar system was not nearly as thick as that in Earth's solar system, nor was it as dense. In order to make this a fair test, they were approaching the belt at an oblique angle that would cause them to spend a minimum of an hour traversing the densest part of the swarm.

That first course deflection was merely the beginning. All too quickly the asteroids were flying past them at distances of fifty meters or less. Pias's hands were playing across his console like those of a concert pianist at a keyboard. This was where all his training was coming in handy. He had spent every spare moment for the last few months practicing at these controls. The intellectual knowledge of where each control was located on the board was of no use; his fingers had to know their way there by instinct, had to make the proper adjustments—no more, no less—by sheer eye-to-hand coordination, bypassing the conscious mind completely. The problem was immeasurably complicated by the fact that he was dealing with three dimensions rather than two; he had to worry, not only about right and left, forward and back, but also up and down.

Each correction he made altered the relative paths of the other rocks around him so that their new courses had to be checked. Sometimes his changes actually brought him into danger from asteroids that would have missed by a wide margin if he hadn't swerved to avoid a previous one.

There was sweat on his forehead and a drop trickled down into his eye, burning it. He tried to blink it away; he dared not take his hands from the control board long enough to wipe at it. For a while he was piloting with only one good eye, which diminished his depth perception and made his movements slightly less reliable. After a few moments his eye watered sufficiently to dilute the sweat and the discomfort eased. It was to his credit that not once during that time did Jules make a move to take control away from him.

Then they were through the worst part of the belt, and Pias's breathing started returning to normal. He made a casual maneuver to slide gracefully away from one approaching asteroid—and suddenly found himself facing an onrushing behemoth head on. It appeared out of nowhere on the scanner and came straight toward him at a speed nearly equal to his own.

If Pias had stopped to think, he and Jules might have ended up as slime on the face of the space rock. His hands moved with a life of their own, swerving the ship's direction so quickly that he was nearly knocked out of his chair. He imagined he could hear the asteroid scraping along the side of the ship as they passed one another, even though the distance was nearly ten meters. Out of the corner of his eye, he could see Jules's hands poised over the co-pilot's controls; the more experienced man would have taken over in another fraction of a second—but even that might have been too late.

Then abruptly they were out of the zone and into what was considered open space again. The sensors indicated completely empty space ahead, so Pias reduced speed, switched on the autopilot once more, and sagged limply back in his seat.

"Must have been a rogue," Jules said calmly beside him. "Most of the asteroids within the zone are moving approximately in the same direction and speed. Occasionally a free one gets captured moving the other way. It doesn't usually last too long because it collides with the rocks going the other way, just like it nearly collided with us."

Pias paused to regain his breath, then asked, "Well, how'd I do?"

"We're alive and unscratched—that's all that really matters. The Service doesn't give points for neatness." He smiled as he added, "Next time, of course, you'll have to practice dodging while firing back at them at the same time."

"You're so encouraging." Pias plotted the course back to DesPlaines and spent the next two hours relaxing after his ordeal.

Landings, as he had learned, were the hardest part of flying any air or spacecraft—particularly landings on a three-gee world where the ground comes up to meet you at a dizzying speed. This was the maneuver he'd practiced most often, and it still made him slightly nervous. He moved with special care as he brought the ship down to a perfect landing on the small private spaceport field that adjoined Felicité, the ducal manor house of the d'Alembert family. As the two men climbed out of the ship, a groundcar pulled up to the edge of the field and their wives waved at them.

Yvette Bavol and Vonnie d'Alembert were the other halves of what were acknowledged to be the two best undercover teams in the Service of the Empire. All four were high-grav natives, with all the speed, strength, and agility that implied. All four were intelligent and resourceful, highly trained, and highly motivated. In addition, Jules and his sister Yvette were members of the extraordinary Family d'Alembert, with its tradition of loyalty and devotion to the Empire and its rulers.

"I see you both made it back intact," Vonnie shouted as the groundcar drove onto the landing field to meet the two men.

The car pulled to a stop and each of the spacefarers kissed his wife in greeting. "How can you ladies have ever doubted me?" Pias asked immodestly.

"I had no doubt whatsoever that you'd brag about it afterwards," his wife laughed. "It was the part in between takeoff and landing that worried us."

"I had to teach him *something*," Jules said. "There's only so many times you can save the Empire on dumb luck alone."

The incident he referred to had happened six months ago during the coronation of Empress Stanley Eleven, while the forces of Lady A's conspiracy had been massing to attack Earth. Pias, alone in a space vessel he didn't know how to pilot, had been the only one in position to warn the Imperial Fleet that they were heading for an ambush. He'd accomplished the feat by pushing buttons at random and piloting his craft in the most absurd way possible so that the Imperial Fleet stopped short of the ambush site to investigate.

It was an achievement of special daring—but afterwards, all concerned agreed that it would be best if, in the future, the young Gospodin Bavol learned how to fly a spacecraft accurately. They'd been fortunate that, because of the rout of the conspiracy's forces, there was a quiet period with no assignments, giving Pias time to learn the needed skills.

His intensified course under Jules's watchful eye had made him into a very good pilot in a surprisingly short time.

The four young people were laughing as they climbed into the groundcar for the short ride to the manor house itself. The past few months had been a welcome and much needed vacation after the strenuous assignments that culminated with the coronation. The entire Empire had been shaken by the bold attack on Earth, but it had held on and had not toppled. There followed a period of peace that allowed everyone a chance to breathe more easily—even though the agents knew such a state of affairs could not last forever.

The call they'd feared came that very night, after they finished dinner. The frequency and the coding of the subetheric transmission left no doubt that the call came from the Head of the Service himself. The d'Alemberts and the Bavols adjourned quickly to the mansion's com room to receive their assignments in privacy.

There, seated in upholstered leather chairs around a large table with built-in computer terminals, they acknowledged receipt of the signal. The decoding device unscrambled the incoming message and a shape slowly materialized in the air above the center of the table—the familiar face of Grand Duke Zander von Wilmenhorst, Head of the Service of the Empire.

The Grand Duke's most striking feature was that his head was completely shaven, giving a dramatic effect to the lean, lined face. A closer observer, however, would notice the brightness in his eyes, a depth of keen intelligence that was restive, ever thinking. The Head was relentless in his pursuit of the Empire's enemies; now in his fiftieth year, he combined his native intellect with long experience, and though comparatively few within the Empire knew the crucial role he played in its affairs, he was regarded in the highest echelons as the government's premier strategist.

The agents were prepared to greet their boss cheerfully, but the grim expression on the Head's face made them realize something was seriously amiss. Dispensing with the usual formalities, Jules asked quickly, "What's wrong?"

"We've been wondering what little game the conspiracy would play next, after their defeat on Coronation Day," von Wilmenhorst said. "We had the Service braced for almost anything, anywhere, and still they've managed to surprise us. They've launched an attack against the Service itself using the most diabolical, insidious weapon they could find."

"I almost hate to ask, but what is it?" Yvette said.

"You," the Head replied. As the agents stared back at him, perplexed, he added, "Or rather, some people impersonating you."

"How can they?" Vonnie asked. "Nobody knows what we look like."

"That's precisely what they're counting on," the Head told them. "Fifty-five days ago, the Service headquarters on Bolshaya received a high priority call that all the local agents were supposed to gather at a remote location for an important assignment. The chief officer on Bolshaya logged the call into his records, exactly as he was supposed to, and assembled his people according to instructions. When we heard nothing from Bolshaya for several days, we had agents from nearby Rellan go over to investigate. It seems our personnel on Bolshaya were ambushed and massacred— all of them. They were *not* inexperienced people; the only reason they walked into the ambush without the slightest suspicion was because the call came from Agents Wombat and Periwinkle."

Jules and Yvette exploded with indignation. "We were never anywhere near there!" Jules exclaimed, and Yvette added, "We've been here on DesPlaines for the last six months."

"I know all that," the Head nodded. "Let me continue. Precisely twenty-six days later, on Blodgett, events repeated themselves. All the agents except one, who was in the hospital recovering from surgery, were lured to a remote location and slaughtered by two people claiming to be Wombat and Periwinkle. Then three days ago—exactly twenty-six days after the massacre on Blodgett—the same thing happened on Arcta."

"I don't like having our names taken in vain." Anyone who knew Jules could have told from the cold fury in his voice that *someone* was going to pay heavily.

"And *I* don't like the fact that fifty-three good, decent people were senselessly murdered simply for serving the cause of justice," the Head told them. His anger was not as visible as Jules's, but his voice was equally determined. "I know you're not involved in this—if you wanted to betray the Service you could have thought of better and subtler ways. But we cannot allow this imposture to continue."

"I presume you want us to take care of it," Pias said.

The Head paused, a rare trace of indecision on his face. "That's what I called to discuss. I'm not completely sure that would be the right thing to do. As I see it, this whole maneuver is a trap aimed specifically at Jules and Yvette."

"How can you tell?" Vonnie asked.

"We know the conspiracy has been tapped into our information for some time. They know a great deal about us, but I don't think they know absolutely everything. They do know the agents codenamed Wombat and Periwinkle are the two best we have, and that there are standing orders for everyone in the field to give them the utmost, unquestioning cooperation. But I don't think they know your identities, because *that* is not generally known;

to the best of my knowledge it's never been written down or entered in any records. We thought this would be the safest course of action; it gave you total anonymity to act as you felt necessary, yet it gave you access to the Service's resources when you needed them.

"Lady A wants to destroy your effectiveness, either by handicapping your operations or by killing you outright. Look at the choices we have open to us:

"We could do nothing at all, in which case they'd probably go on wiping out station after station. That is unacceptable; too many people have already died because of this subterfuge.

"Or we could put out the order that anyone identifying themselves as Wombat or Periwinkle should be shot on sight. That would keep our agents from being duped by the imposters, but it wouldn't make your job very easy. If we gave you new codenames, there's no guarantee the conspiracy wouldn't learn them and pull the same trick over again.

"Or we could take a middle tack by saying that orders from Wombat and Periwinkle need not be obeyed unquestioningly. We could either circulate your description or make the local branches more reluctant to give you assistance—but that would hamper *your* activities. Any of these choices would end up restricting your effectiveness in some way that could only benefit the conspiracy."

"There's another solution," Yvette said. "You could send us out to get them. We're the only agents who wouldn't be fooled because we know who the real Wombat and Periwinkle are."

The Head sighed. "Yes, that thought occurred to me, too. But that's exactly what Lady A wants. Just look at the pattern. Each of the three systems hit so far is about ten parsecs away from the previous one along a straight line. The events are spaced exactly twenty-six days apart, and the method is the same in each case. It's ridiculously easy to predict where, when, and how they will strike next. They might as well put up a gigantic sign advertising themselves. And they know that only the *real* Wombat and Periwinkle could challenge their impostors without hesitation. They'll be waiting for you."

"In a way," Jules said, "it's flattering to think they'd go to so much trouble just for us."

"I could do very nicely without such flattery," his sister commented. "Particularly when I think we're indirectly responsible for the deaths of fifty-three of our fellow agents. If it weren't for the system established to help us, they'd still be alive today."

"There you have it," von Wilmenhorst said. "I admit to being in a bit of a quandary. I know what I'd *like* to do—but I hate playing into that woman's hands. I'd like your opinions on this matter; it could affect either your jobs or your lives."

"In large measure," Yvette said, "our jobs *are* our lives. I can't speak for Jules, but I don't want to give in to sneaky blackmail like this."

"You can speak for me, and very well," Jules said. "I agree completely. We *have* to prove to Lady A and her *mokoes* that they can't laugh in our faces. They manipulated us badly on our last encounter; we can't let them do that again."

"But isn't that exactly what they *are* doing?" Pias pointed out. "Don't you think they're counting on our pride to make us come straight to them?"

"Pias is right," the Head said. "I think that's exactly what they're banking on. They know our reactions entirely too well and they're setting us up."

"Still," Yvette said, "as you yourself admitted, what other choice do we have? If we give in here, they'll only put pressure on us somewhere else. They'll push us back and back until we have no farther to go. If the line is going to be drawn at all, we might as well draw it now.

"Besides," she added, "they may force the direction we're going in, but they can't always guess how fast or how far we'll go. Lady A has miscalculated before, remember."

"So have we," Pias muttered, but the others pretended not to hear him.

The Head talked to them for a little while longer, giving them the pertinent details of the case. He signed off with the Service toast, "Here's to tomorrow, fellows and friends. May we all live to see it!" He acted as though this were just an ordinary assignment, even though no case the d'Alemberts and Bavols worked on could be called ordinary.

But this one was special, and all four knew it. For the first time they would be walking into a trap designed specifically for them; they would need courage, strength, and not a little luck to escape this particular menace.

3
The Trail To C

Captain Paul Fortier of Naval Intelligence hadn't allowed himself the luxury of a six-month vacation after the attack against Earth on Coronation Day. He'd been offered a long vacation and an important assignment at Luna Base, but he'd asked that they be postponed. He'd been in the middle of a long-standing assignment, to destroy the pirate network, when the emergency to the Empire occurred. Even though he'd dealt spectacularly with the invasion, he considered his work incomplete. The pirates had been dispersed and their major operations disbanded, but there were still loose ends to be wrapped up. He was the person with the most intimate knowledge of the pirates' operations, having worked undercover in their organization for several years, and so he was the logical choice to supervise the mopping up. The Imperial Navy, proud of his dedication, agreed to give him the opportunity.

Under the name "Rocheville," Fortier had worked his way up to being one of pirate leader Shen Tzu's chief lieutenants. As such, he had detailed information about many of the people the pirates dealt with on the local level, planet to planet; and much of what he didn't know was supplied by the pirates' own records when their base was captured. Now he was set on tracking down those intermediaries, making sure they'd be put away where they couldn't hurt society again.

The pirate network had been widespread, and Fortier's job was vast. He could not do it all himself. Instead, he was put in charge of a task force, with five other officers of Naval Intelligence working under him. The group worked in cooperation with planetary police forces, and Fortier coordinated the joint effort. He chafed at this; he had joined Naval Intelligence because he enjoyed the adventure of work in the field, and he hated being stuck behind a desk. He therefore took every opportunity to get out and do some of the actual work himself.

When the pirates had been smashed, their contacts, realizing that they would now be wanted by the law, tried to vanish into the regular criminal underground that existed on nearly every civilized planet. Some were more successful at this than others. Many of them had been legitimate businessmen except for their dealings with the pirates, and weren't familiar with the criminal networks. They were picked up almost immediately. The tougher ones were those with previous criminal records, with long experience at hiding from the authorities. These required dogged determination to track down—a quality that was fortunately not lacking in Fortier and his people.

It was in a dimly lit, foul-smelling bar on the planet Lateesta that a major breakthrough occurred. Fortier and his police contact, Detective Nikopolous, had staked out the underworld hangout on a tip that Fortier's fugitive, a man named Guitirrez, would be there that evening. They waited a while and, as predicted, Guitirrez entered the bar and sat down alone at one of the battered tables. He looked as though he might be waiting for someone; he kept glancing at the door and checking the time. In view of this behavior, Fortier and Nikopolous decided not to arrest Guitirrez immediately; he might inadvertently lead them to bigger fish in his scummy pond.

Their hunch paid off. Forty-five minutes later, a woman joined Guitirrez at his table. She was Junoesque, in her early fifties, with graying hair, and a hard expression on her face. Neither Fortier nor Nikopolous had ever seen her before, but Fortier made sure to snap several pictures of her with his tiny hidden camera.

The meeting broke up after a few minutes. Guitirrez sat nursing his drink while the woman got up and left the bar. Fortier left his associate to tend to the routine task of arresting Guitirrez; he was much more interested in tailing this mysterious woman to find out more about her. She might be just a routine friend of Guitirrez, having no connection to any illegal activities—but Fortier was not one to give up on a lead until it was proved to be false.

The woman walked briskly to the nearest tubeway station; Fortier was hard pressed to keep pace with her and not make himself conspicuous at the same time. He just managed to catch the same turbotrain, staying as far away from her in the car as possible and making sure to avoid eye contact. She sat calmly as the turbotrain rode through several stations, and Fortier was able to rely on his peripheral vision to let him know when she made any moves.

She got off the tubeway where it connected to the monoliner station and went immediately into the ladies' restroom. Fortier cursed his luck and used his personal minicom to call for a female assistant as backup. The monoliner station security had a woman officer to him within three minutes, and he sent her in to check the restroom. The woman he'd been tailing was not there.

This particular lavatory had two entrances, one from the station and one from the street. The woman had obviously gone out the second door and given him the slip. She could be anywhere by now.

Dejected at his failure, Fortier returned to police headquarters, where Guitirrez was being held for interrogation. Although it didn't take much effort to get Guitirrez to admit his part in the piracy, he insisted he knew nothing about the woman he'd met in the bar. He'd been told to call a certain number whenever he was in trouble. He'd done so on several previous occasions and had been given instructions on how to hide out safely. On this last occasion, the person at the other end had told him to wait in this bar for a woman who'd give him further orders. The woman had come as promised and told him a ticket off-planet in the name of Martinez was waiting for him at the spaceport. He'd been arrested before he could leave the bar and pick up the ticket. That was all he claimed to know about the matter.

The police did what they could to verify the man's story. There was indeed a starship ticket at the spaceport reserved in the name of Martinez; it would have taken the fugitive halfway across the Empire and might have helped him elude capture for a considerable time. The vidiphone number had been assigned to a name that turned out to be fictitious, and there was no way to trace it to anyone. The police even gave Guitirrez a shot of detrazine, the strongest legal truth serum known, but his story remained the same.

Fortier decided to concentrate on the woman who'd met Guitirrez in the bar. She was obviously a connection to higher, more important channels. He passed the photos around within the detective division, but no one could ever recall having seen her before. Copies of the pictures were made and circulated to all police personnel on Lateesta.

Descriptions were sent to all spaceport security people to prevent the woman from leaving the planet, although Fortier was convinced he was locking the barn door after the rustling. In the meantime, he locked himself away in an office, spread the photos across the top of the empty desk, and studied them himself to pry loose any pertinent information he could.

After staring hopelessly at the pictures for a while, his eye noticed a detail it had missed before. It was very tiny, and he ordered the photos enlarged to see it more clearly. The enlargements showed the mysterious woman wearing around her neck a thin gold chain that held a small integrated circuit chip dangling from its center.

In the past few months since the near disaster on Coronation Day, NI and SOTE had buried most of their interservice rivalry. A great deal of information was now flowing between the two organizations, and one of the items SOTE strongly stressed to Naval Intelligence was that there was a well-organized conspiracy trying to topple the Stanley dynasty. One of its recognition symbols was a necklace just like the one this mysterious lady was wearing. Ever since the attack on Earth it was known that the pirates had been somehow involved with this conspiracy— but this development led to new, and perhaps unexpected, connections. It was certainly worth checking further.

Even as he was congratulating himself on spotting that tiny detail, Fortier received his second big break on the case. A call arrived for him from none other than the Superintendent of Police for Lateesta. "I just had a chance to look at the photos you circulated, and I must say I was shocked to see her here in a cheap bar associating with known criminals this way."

"You can identify the woman, then?" Fortier asked eagerly.

"Certainly," the Superintendent said. "I spoke with her

just three months ago at a law enforcement symposium on Corian. That's Elsa Helmund, Commissioner of Police for the planet Durward.''

Fortier did not have a ship of his own available, and had to settle for commercial transportation. He booked passage on the next connecting flights to Durward, inwardly fuming that it would take a full nine days to reach his destination. He could have made a subetheric call ahead and had the investigation started by local officials, but Elsa Helmund was so highly placed and the case against her was so tentative he didn't dare risk spooking her. The Commissioner of Police for an entire planet would be a major cog in the conspiracy's machinery, and she might lead to other important members. The more people who knew what he was after, the more chance there'd be a leak.

For obvious reasons he did not contact the Durward police to let them know he'd be coming. He *did* let the local SOTE office know, and they promised him the utmost cooperation when he arrived. For now, he trusted no one but himself with the possibility that Elsa Helmund was a traitor.

On reaching Durward he checked in with SOTE immediately. The local Service chief tried to be helpful. She called for the files on Elsa Helmund, but was bluntly informed that those files were classified, and only people with an F-17 security clearance or higher would be allowed to see it. That excluded her.

Fortier, however, had a G-8 security rating. He inserted his identity card and comparison disc, then put his eyes to the retinascope so the machine could verify him. His identity was acknowledged but the machine still refused to yield the desired information. When Fortier demanded an explanation, the computer indicated that such information had been erased from the memory.

Furious, Fortier turned to the SOTE chief and asked if she had any personal knowledge of Helmund's background. "She's been Police Commissioner here for about ten years, and she seems to have done a good job," the woman said. "I've met her briefly at a couple of official functions. I do know she's not native to Durward. She came specifically for the post of Police Commissioner. The competition was open to outsiders—the Duke wanted the best person he could find, and Elsa Helmund filled the bill. Her references said she'd had a long, distinguished career with the police on her native world, Preis; she also had letters of reference—I *know* I've got copies of those—from both the Grand Duke of Sector Four and his Sector Marshal that were glowing with praise. She was far and away the best qualified candidate, so she got the job. As far as I know, there've been no complaints about her performance."

"Can you get hold of her file from Preis for me?" Fortier asked.

"Why the sudden interest in Gospozha Helmund?"

In answer, Fortier showed her photos of Helmund with the necklace clearly visible. The SOTE officer asked no further questions. "It may take a few hours to get what we need," she apologized.

"That's smooth," Fortier said grimly. "I'll wait."

The information from Preis, when it finally did arrive, was equally frustrating. There simply *was* no information about anyone named Elsa Helmund—no record of her birth, no record of her having worked for the police department there, no record of anyone matching that description ever even existing on the planet.

"I think it's time I had a talk with Gospozha Helmund," Fortier mused, and the officer from SOTE agreed.

Fortier called Helmund's office, only to be told that the Commissioner had been away on vacation for the past three weeks and was expected back tomorrow. Fortier decided to make a surreptitious visit to Helmund's home before the woman returned.

The apartment was quite normal. Elsa Helmund lived alone and had simple tastes. The only thing at all out of the ordinary was a telecom unit and teletype connected to a computer terminal in the wall—a link-up that had the potential to connect her with anyone in the Galaxy. In a wastebasket beside the teleprinter was a burned scrap of paper that Fortier took back to SOTE headquarters. "Can you do anything with this?" he asked them.

The SOTE technicians were miracle workers. Though the scrap, to the naked eye, was little more than a flimsy piece of charcoal, they were able to differentiate between the plain paper and the chemicals that had gone into the ink printed on it. Some of the words were completely burned away, but enough was there to make out the name Guitirrez, the planet Lateesta, and something about a ticket. The note was signed with the single initial, C.

The Police Commissioner did not show up in her office the next day as her aides expected. Fortier guessed that someone or something must have tipped her off. Elsa Helmund would not be returning to her office, ever. There was no point waiting around here.

Fortier's next port of call was Preis, the capital planet of Sector Four. It seemed odd to him that someone could come to a strange place with such blatantly false credentials. It also disturbed him greatly that the Grand Duke and the Sector Marshal for all of Sector Four would have written such extravagant praise for someone who, according to official records, did not exist. Fortier was determined to find out why, and whether those people, too, were part of the conspiracy.

The Grand Duke for this sector, like many other Grand

Dukes, spent much of his time back on Earth at the center of Imperial administration. He was thus unavailable to be interviewed. The Sector Marshal, a man named Herman Stanck, was scarcely less difficult to get hold of. As the chief administrative officer of one of the most populous sectors of the Empire, he was responsible for overseeing the harmonious government of scores of planets as well as the relationship between Sector Four and all the other sectors. Fortier had to use every bit of influence he had just to be granted a five-minute interview with the Sector Marshal.

Stanck's office was spacious and comfortable. The back wall was one large picture window looking out over the capital city of Aachen; the other walls held series of shelves filled with enough bookreels to put any library to shame. Stanck's enormous solentawood desk was crowded but orderly. There were several chairs and a couch grouped about the desk.

Stanck seemed out of place in such a comfortable office, a brusque man with thinning brown hair and a hawk nose. He greeted Fortier with a brisk handshake and guided him to a chair. "Well, Captain, what can I do for you?" he asked as he sat down behind his desk.

Fortier had to be discreet. He had no direct evidence against this man, and if he moved too far too fast he could be in serious trouble. "I know your time is valuable, sir, so I'll be brief. What do you know of Elsa Helmund?"

"I don't recall the name offhand."

"In a letter of reference you gave her, you called her a close personal friend and the most efficient police official you'd ever known."

Stanck shook his head. "I have no memory of ever doing so."

"You deny writing the letter, then?"

"How long ago was this, Captain?"

"Ten years."

Stanck leaned forward in his seat. "Do you have any idea, Captain, how many people I meet and deal with every day, let alone over a ten-year period? I have to keep my mind free of clutter; if I don't deal with a name on a frequent basis I forget about it or store it in my files. I may very well have written the letter you claim I did. I simply have no recollection of it."

Fortier handed him a copy of the letter. "Is that your signature?"

Stanck glanced at it, then handed the document back. "It looks like it. Either that or a very good forgery."

"If you had written this letter, would you have a copy in your files?"

"Most likely. I keep permanent records of everything I do."

"May I see those records, please?"

"No, you may not." Stanck's tone became even more brusque. "I am not in the habit of letting strangers roam at will through my private files. Those records are kept for my benefit alone. Some of them are highly confidential. They are not public records, and no one but me has the right to examine them."

"Gospodin Stanck, this is a matter of the highest Imperial security. . . ."

"Then may I suggest you proceed through the proper channels? Unless, of course," Stanck's eyebrows narrowed, "you're accusing me of some impropriety, in which case you'll find I make a very formidable enemy."

Fortier refused to be intimidated. "So do I, sir."

"The time for your audience is up, Captain." Stanck buzzed for one of his aides to come and escort Fortier from the room. "If we meet another time," was his parting shot, "you had better come armed with more than sly innuendos."

I will, Stanck, I will, Fortier thought with determination.

For the next few days, Herman Stanck became an obsession with Fortier. He pored over the man's lengthy file in the SOTE computers until he'd virtually memorized it. In fifteen years of service as Sector Marshal, Stanck's record was unblemished. A dedicated public servant, he had never married, preferring to devote his entire life to the administration of Sector Four's affairs. There were many newsroll accounts of his public actions, and a long list of awards and honors he'd received. His private life was kept strictly private, but there'd never been the breath of a scandal— and that in itself was some kind of a record for a man who'd served in public life as long as Stanck.

To all appearances, the Sector Marshal was as loyal as anyone could wish. Accusing him of treason would be like strangling orphans or drowning kittens; Fortier dared not move against him until he had strong proof on his side. And yet, an undercover agent lived by his instincts—and all of Fortier's well-trained intuition told him Stanck's hostility masked some guilty secret. It was inconceivable to Fortier that a man could write such a glowing report about someone and not remember it later, even after ten busy years—particularly when that person had never existed in the first place.

There were no clues in Stanck's professional record, so Fortier dug even more deeply into the man's personal file. Stanck was a solitary sort, and no one knew him really well. There was nothing in these files, either, that would mark him as a traitor.

In desperation, Fortier turned to the financial report. Stanck lived modestly, well within his means. He didn't gamble or squander his salary, and had made some shrewd investments that left him a reasonably wealthy man—but there was no indication of any impropriety there, just sound business dealings. Fortier was about to abandon this avenue of inquiry too when his eye noticed one small, obscure detail that almost escaped notice because it was so hidden. Stanck's assets revealed that he was, upon retirement, owed a fortune in sick leave pay because it had accumulated without being used.

Fortier called up the pay records, and they told an amazing story. In the fifteen years that Stanck had been Sector Marshal, he had not missed a day of work because of illness. There were no records of any sort before Stanck took the job, merely the cryptic entry that the man had been appointed especially by the Grand Duke.

These were anomalies that Fortier could sink his teeth into. For the second time in this case, he'd run into someone with no past. He was even more intrigued by Stanck's phenomenal health. It would be incredible enough for a man in his early twenties—but for someone in his middle years, it was downright unbelievable.

Fortier asked for the medical records on his subject, only to find that there weren't any. Stanck had never visited a doctor in all the years he'd been Sector Marshal. Under normal circumstances, every public employee had to undergo a physical examination before being hired, but a cryptic note on Stanck's file said that this requirement had been waived in his case by direct order of the Grand Duke.

An idea was forming in Fortier's mind, one he didn't like a bit. He knew all too well that the conspiracy was capable of creating robot duplicates of people and substituting them for the real ones; he himself had been impersonated by a robot during the few months preceding the attack against Earth, and the experience had nearly been fatal. What if Stanck were such a robot, infiltrated into the management of Sector Four? It would explain why he'd never been ill and why he'd never gone to see a doctor. It would explain the man's solitary lifestyle, his precise and punctual work habits—and his hostility to anyone like Fortier who tried to peer too closely into his background.

If Stanck was indeed a robot he would have to be handled very cautiously. The robots had superhuman strength and were immune to stun weapons. Only a blaster would bring a robot down, and it could cause untold destruction if not controlled quickly once its identity was uncovered.

The first step was to prove conclusively that Stanck was a robot. The local SOTE office was most cooperative about providing Fortier with the long range sensor equipment he asked for, and the naval officer set about the difficult task of getting readings on Stanck's body. The trouble was that Stanck rarely went out in public. He was either in his office, in his car, or in his apartment—places where it was difficult for Fortier's equipment to get a clear reading uncluttered by surroundings.

After a week, Fortier's patience paid off. Stanck was scheduled to give a speech at the local sports stadium before a series of charity games. Fortier attended, and was able to get close enough to train his instruments on the Sector Marshal. The readings confirmed Fortier's worst suspicions: Stanck was not a living human being, but a complex artificial mechanism covered with plastiderm. All of Sector Four was being administered by a robot agent of the deadly conspiracy.

Fortier weighed his next moves very carefully. He was out of his depth in this matter, and he knew it. Tracking down treason was really SOTE's business; Naval Intelligence was responsible for rooting out pirates, smugglers, and other miscreants who used the spaceways for illegal purposes. In all honesty, he should have turned the case over to SOTE when he had discovered the Helmund connection, but his teeth were too solidly into it to let go; he wanted to keep with this matter now to its conclusion.

Consequently he did not inform SOTE of his newly-found information. Instead, he went to the local naval station and recruited some colleagues to capture the robot.

They approached Stanck one morning in his underground garage just as he was getting into his groundcar to go to the office. As an important official, Stanck had a cluster of bodyguards around him; Fortier had taken the precaution of bringing with him a squad of twenty Planetary Patrolmen. As the two groups approached one another amid the concrete pillars of the underground garage, tension developed instantly.

"Hold it, Stanck," Fortier called. "You're not going anywhere."

"You have no jurisdiction here, Captain," the other said icily. "If your people don't back away instantly, I'll have you court-martialed so fast your circuits will fuse."

"I know you're a robot," Fortier continued despite the threat. "You're part of a conspiracy to overthrow the Stanley dynasty."

"I've been accused of many things in my time, but that's the most ridiculous charge I've ever heard." Stanck turned his back on the officer and started to enter his car.

Fortier gave a signal, and his group suddenly drew their weapons. This brought an immediate reaction from the Sector Marshal's bodyguards, and within seconds the air was filled with the sounds of a stun-gun battle. The robot, however, did not wait to observe the outcome. It slipped into the car and sped hastily away from the scene of the battle before anyone could stop it.

Captain Fortier, too, hurried away, leaving the fighting to his comrades. He had not intended to capture Stanck just yet; he was hoping to panic it into making some hasty mistake. In a direct confrontation, the robot would have allowed him to destroy it rather than tell him anything— and, with its strength and immunity to stun-guns, there was almost no way to capture it "alive." His only hope was that the robot would lead him to yet a bigger connection before he was forced to destroy it.

Fortier had a copter waiting hidden on the street a block away. The pilot saw him coming and revved up the motor, so they were able to take off the instant Fortier jumped into the passenger seat. Within seconds they were airborne and ready to follow the robot's car wherever it might lead them. Fortier cautioned the pilot not to get too close; they didn't want the robot to realize it was being tailed.

The Sector Marshal's groundcar had an automatic priority device, damping the motors of surrounding cars to let it pass by them unhindered. It sped out of Aachen in record time, the robot trusting to its computer-fast reflexes to drive more recklessly than any human would dare. Even in a copter Fortier had trouble keeping up, and he no longer had to caution his pilot to hang back. They had to fly at top speed if they didn't want to lose their quarry.

Out in the open countryside, the robot drove even faster. The car was practically a blur on the highway. But it soon became obvious that its destination was the estate of the Grand Duke himself. Fortier found himself licking his lips. He'd been hoping this was where the trail would lead. The Grand Duke's name had also been on Helmund's references, and it had been at his specific direction that Stanck was hired as Sector Marshal.

Stanck's car was scanned and identified, so it drove through the grounds of the estate unimpeded, screeching to a halt before the large doors of the main house. The robot jumped out of the car and disappeared into the mansion just as Fortier's copter was coming in for a quick landing.

The Grand Duke's guards came running out to inspect this unknown intruder. Fortier had his identity card out and flashed it at the security officers. "Naval Intelligence," he shouted urgently. "The Sector Marshal is a fugitive and an impostor. We can't let him get away!"

The conflicts in their loyalties, both to the Grand Duke and to the Empire, caused the guards to hesitate as they tried to decide whether to stop this intruder or help him. That slight pause was all Fortier needed to dodge past them and slip through the doors. He had his blaster drawn, prepared for any surprises the robot might throw at him.

He caught a fleeting glimpse of the robot turning left at the far end of the long marble corridor ahead, and he raced in pursuit. When he reached the crossing hallway where the sector marshal had turned, his quarry had vanished from sight. There were, however, some startled servants standing mystified at Stanck's hurried flight. Fortier ran to the nearest one and flashed his ID card again. "I'm Captain Fortier, Naval Intelligence. Stanck is a traitor to the Empire and a fugitive. Which way did he go?"

The woman was a bit flustered at the odd events of the last few seconds. "He . . . he went into the security council chamber over there."

Fortier ran to the indicated door, but found it locked. The door itself was carved wood reinforced with magnisteel. The woman who'd pointed the way explained, "No one is permitted in there except the Grand Duke and the Sector Marshal. The door opens only to their touch."

Fortier gave no thought to the consequences of what he was doing. He knew he was already committed to the largest gamble of his career. If he was wrong about any of his assumptions, court-martial would be the least serious thing that would happen to him. Grand Dukes were the highest rank of nobility below the Empress herself. By invading this estate without legal authority, he'd put his neck on the block and sharpened the blade for the headsman; the only excuse he could offer for his various improprieties was that he'd been in "hot pursuit." It would be a feeble excuse if his guesses were wrong.

With so much already at stake, there was no point in

letting a door stand in his way. Aiming his blaster point blank at the lock, he burned through it in just a second and pushed the door inward with a loud crash.

The Sector Marshal was bent over a computer terminal by a desk at the far side of the room. It looked up as Fortier came charging in, and reached to its side, as though for a weapon. The naval officer did not hesitate, firing his blaster with deadly accuracy at the robot's chest. The blazing beam sizzled through the air and struck the treacherous creation on target. The robot lurched backward against the wall, then slumped quietly to the ground.

Fortier walked over to the desk and examined the terminal where the robot had been working. It looked as though Stanck had been trying to erase certain information and documents from the memory files, but had not yet had time to complete the job. Fortier called up those files; it took only a casual glance at their contents to realize he'd been correct in his assumptions. The Grand Duke was personally involved in this conspiracy.

The Captain looked up to find himself staring into the muzzle of a blaster being wielded by the Grand Duke's chief of security. "You killed the Sector Marshal," the man said.

"Check that more closely," Fortier replied. "The being you thought was Herman Stanck was a robot, a tool of a galaxy-wide conspiracy to overthrow the Stanley dynasty. Furthermore, if you'll look at this display, there's evidence against the Grand Duke himself."

The security chief had one of his guards verify the information about Stanck, then he read the display on the computer terminal over Fortier's shoulder. His eyes slowly widened in astonishment, and he lowered his gun. Fortier relaxed with relief, but did not let it show.

"Go back to business as normal," he told the security chief. "Under no circumstances should you inform the

Grand Duke of what's happened here until I consult my superiors and decide what to do.''

The security chief nodded and ordered his people back to their duties. He himself backed slowly out of the room, leaving Fortier alone.

The captain spent the next half hour checking the files, becoming more and more awed by how high an official he had reached within the criminal organization. The computer memory banks contained names, dates, places—all sorts of records that would totally demolish the conspiracy's forces. There were cryptic entries about a woman known only as Lady A, and the indication that the Grand Duke signed himself with the codename of C.

The time had come for Fortier to bring his superiors into the case. He had gone as far as he could on his own authority—and actually quite a bit beyond. He dared not move against anyone as highly placed as a Grand Duke, even on evidence as tight as this, without backup from Luna Base.

He was not surprised to find a subcom unit built into this office. This was obviously one of the nerve centers for the conspiracy, and the Grand Duke would want to stay in touch with developments all over the Galaxy. Fortier used that same subcom set to beam a message back to Admiral Trejas, Director of Naval Intelligence, at Luna Base.

Fortier had to bull his way past innumerable secretaries and aides by insisting his information was important enough for Admiral Trejas to deal with it personally. Fortunately, he had enough of a reputation from his heroic actions during the Coronation Day Incursion that he was listened to, and eventually he got Admiral Trejas personally on the line.

Captain Fortier gave his superior a carefully edited version of his story. One reason for the editing was that the call was not being scrambled, and he didn't want the information spread about too quickly; another was that he wanted to gloss over some of his own more unorthodox behavior. Nevertheless, he was able to give his superior an accurate rundown of his activities and a summary of the evidence he'd uncovered.

The admiral's eyes widened at the mention of C and the linkage with the Grand Duke of Sector Four. "Are you positive of your facts?" he asked the captain again.

Fortier could only repeat the information he had discovered within the Grand Duke's very household.

Admiral Trejas rubbed his forehead and sighed. *"Khorosho,* I believe you. But we can't act too hastily in this matter. Moving against a Grand Duke is a serious undertaking. I'll have to get authorization from higher up."

"If you get the authorization," Fortier said, "I'd like to be in on the arrest, if possible."

"I'll get back to you as quickly as I can," the admiral promised as he broke the connection. Then he leaned back in his chair and contemplated the terrible burden that had fallen on his shoulders.

Arresting a Grand Duke for treason would be a difficult proposition in any case. But this was infinitely worse, because Admiral Trejas was one of a small number of people who knew that the Grand Duke of Sector Four, Zander von Wilmenhorst, was actually the Head of the Service of the Empire. Arresting him would be no slight matter indeed.

4
___ The Arrest of von Wilmenhorst ___

After pausing a few minutes to collect his wits and his courage, Admiral Trejas put in a call to his own superior, Lord Admiral Cesare Benevenuto, the chief military officer of Her Imperial Majesty's Navy. Benevenuto listened to the report with a cold feeling in his heart. Grand Duke Zander was an old and respected acquaintance, but the evidence came from an impeccable source. Benevenuto promised Trejas a quick decision on the matter and promptly placed another call to move the information further up the line.

Except during time of war or Imperial emergency, the Lord Admiral did not report directly to the Empress; instead, protocol demanded that he inform Duke Mosi Burr'uk, currently serving as Prime Councilor of the Imperial Council under Empress Stanley Eleven, just as he had served under her father until her accession to the Imperial Throne six months ago. Although the Empress held full authority, it was the P.C.'s job to screen those items that required her immediate attention and to handle those matters that could be dealt with on a lower level.

The Duke was a small black man in his late fifties. He listened to Benevenuto's report with the same sense of impending fear that the two admirals had felt before him. As Head of SOTE, Zander von Wilmenhorst was also a member of the Imperial Council; he and Duke Mosi had often disagreed on matters of policy, sometimes violently. It galled Burr'uk that Stanley Ten, and now his daughter Edna, seemed to side with von Wilmenhorst more often than with him. Even so, this news hurt him. If it were true that von Wilmenhorst was the mysterious C, it meant there were no Imperial secrets or matters of policy that the conspiracy had not known or shaped. It made him shiver at the thought of how utterly the Empire might have been betrayed.

With no little trepidation, then, Duke Mosi called for an urgent personal meeting with Her Imperial Majesty. Because of the importance of the subject, she agreed to cancel other appointments and see him in half an hour.

The meeting took place in the private conference chamber of the Imperial Palace in Moscow. It was a room designed for work, devoid of the splendor of the more public rooms. Heavy gold and brown velvet tapestries with designs of unicorns and griffins covered the soundproofed walls, dampening noise in here still further. Gilded wooden chairs circled a leather-topped oval conference table that dominated the chamber. It was a coldly majestic place, reflecting the mood of its owner. The Prime Councilor, true to his nature, had arrived early and was waiting respectfully as Edna Stanley, ruler of the Empire of Earth, entered the room.

The Empress, supreme ruler of an empire more vast than any other in human history, was barely twenty-six years old. She was not beautiful, but there was a charm about her appearance that caused most of her subjects to love her on sight. She wore a cream-colored suede jumpsuit and carried herself with royal confidence and pride. If her face was set in severe lines, it was because she bore the heaviest burden mankind had ever devised—total and absolute control over an entire Galaxy.

Edna Stanley took her accustomed seat at the head of the oval table. "Well, my lord," she said to her Prime Councilor, "what have you to say that's so important?"

Duke Mosi made his presentation as simple and understated as he could. The facts were horrifying enough; they needed no elaboration. The Empress listened without once interrupting—a trait she'd picked up from her father—although her face became increasingly drawn and grave as the story unfolded.

She was silent for more than a minute after the Duke had finished his report. The calm expression on her face gave no indication of the war raging within her soul. At last she looked squarely at Burr'uk and said, "You realize, I presume, the seriousness of your accusations."

"No one more so than I, Your Majesty. But I am only repeating what others have reported."

"You've frequently disagreed with Zander at Council meetings. I'm sure you'd appreciate the removal of his opposition."

The Duke's reaction was instantaneous. He approached the Empress' chair and knelt before it with his head bowed. "Your Majesty, our disagreements, while often loud and volatile, have always been honest ones over the best ways to preserve the peace and safety of the Empire. If you think I take any joy in this news, I assure you you are mistaken. Quite the contrary—I'd hate to think our worst enemy has been privy to so many of our secrets. If you think I had some hand in fabricating evidence against Grand Duke Zander, then I hope you'll accept my resignation right now, for a Prime Councilor cannot function without the trust of his sovereign.''

''Get up, Mosi,'' the Empress said. ''My father wouldn't have chosen you as Prime Councilor if he wasn't convinced of your integrity, and I wouldn't have reaffirmed you in the position if *I* had any doubts. I know you'd never stoop to tactics like these just to get rid of someone you disagree with.''

She shook her head. ''It's just that . . . Zander! He's been like a dear uncle to me all my life. It's hard to believe he could be plotting against me.''

The Duke rose and straightened his gold-rimmed glasses. ''The source is Captain Fortier, whom I believe you personally decorated for saving the Empire at your coronation. He emphasized to his superiors that he believes the evidence is unassailable, obtained from the Grand Duke's own files.''

The Empress nodded. ''Perhaps I'm having trouble believing it because I don't *want* to believe it. If Zander *is* C, that means he knows everything about us, all our weak points, all our problems. It also means he has the power to mislead and misdirect us. The Service of the Empire is one of the most powerful tools in our arsenal. It's our eyes and ears. Without it, we'd drift helplessly and the Empire would probably crumble in a matter of months. SOTE is what makes an empire this large possible. . . .''

She shivered and looked directly at the man before her. ''Well, that's peripheral to our problem at the moment. We have a situation that must be dealt with. As my Prime Councilor, what do you recommend we do?''

''I think prudence dictates we operate on the worst possible assumption for the moment—that is, we must assume the information is true and Grand Duke Zander is your archenemy. If so, steps must be taken to neutralize him immediately.''

"I will not condemn him without seeing the evidence firsthand," the Empress insisted.

"Of course not, Your Majesty," Duke Mosi hastily assured her. "I wouldn't do that, either. Arrangements will be made to obtain copies of the incriminating files for our examination as soon as possible. But in the meantime, Grand Duke Zander has intelligence sources of his own, and he is bound to hear what has happened at his own estate. If he is the man behind the conspiracy, he may have some contingency plans that he can set into effect. Since he knows all our weak points, he would know precisely where to act to cripple us most severely. We must put him under arrest immediately and hope to isolate him from his organization. If the evidence later turns out to be false—and I wish it no less than you do—we can release him with our apologies, and no permanent harm is done. If the information is correct, we'll have done what we could to keep him from causing further damage to the Empire."

"No permanent harm," the Empress mused, echoing Duke Mosi's phrase. "I wonder about that. Zander is someone whose trust and friendship I value; there aren't many people I can say that about. How can I accuse him of the highest crimes in the Galaxy, then release him later and expect to keep his loyalty and trust?"

"The Zander von Wilmenhorst I know would understand your position perfectly," the Prime Councilor said. "Were he in my position, he'd be the first to say that Imperial security must rank ahead of friendship."

"You're right about that. But if he is guilty . . ." She paused to consider the ramifications. "If he is guilty, how much of SOTE is in this with him? Helena is his chief assistant; she may be part of the same conspiracy. But the rest of the Service—has he been selecting people who are loyal to him, or to me? If they turn against me, the stability of the Imperial Throne is in serious jeopardy. The matter must be handled with the utmost delicacy.''

"There is another question, Your Majesty,'' Duke Mosi said. "We could not allow the Grand Duke the luxury of a trial, not in a matter this sensitive. If you preside over a High Court of Justice with the other Grand Dukes rendering a verdict, von Wilmenhorst's role as Head of SOTE will have to be revealed. If he is condemned—even if he's the only member of SOTE involved—the organization will have to be completely overhauled. If nothing else, its headquarters will have to be moved out of the Hall of State for Sector Four, where it is now. There will be a period of inevitable turmoil, and there are entirely too many people who'd be willing to take advantage of that. A trial, even *in camera*, would bring out too many things we'd want to keep hidden. You and you alone must decide the case and pronounce sentence.''

The Empress accepted her adviser's opinion thoughtfully, making no immediate comment. Her face was a mask of regal solemnity that gave no indication of the thoughts behind it. "*Khorosho*, my lord. Here are my instructions, which are to be carried out to the letter. Grand Duke Zander von Wilmenhorst and the Duchess Helena are to be placed under house arrest as quickly as possible. There is to be no force used unless they resist arrest, and then only the minimum force needed to carry out orders. They are to be held totally incommunicado, and the case against them must be spelled out to them in detail so they'll have a chance to explain. They are to be treated at all times with the deference and courtesy befitting their ranks. Find out who is number three at SOTE Headquarters. I'll contact that person myself and explain that Zander and Helena are indisposed, and that he is to be in charge until further notice. If we can keep SOTE in the dark about this, at least for a while, it may minimize any threat from that direction.

"If I hear of any unwarranted mistreatment of either Zander or Helena, someone will wish he hadn't been born. I'll take what steps I must to protect the security of the Empire, but I will not hurt two people I love unless the charges against them can be thoroughly proved."

"Yes, Your Majesty. And I'll pray fervently that our worst assumption turns out to be wrong." The Prime Councilor bowed deeply to his sovereign and left the room.

You and I both, Mosi, the Empress thought as she watched him depart.

Edna Stanley had been trained since birth to keep her emotions well hidden in public. First as Crown Princess, and now as Empress, she had known she would be the center of attention. In any difficult situation, people would look to her for a reaction. If she was weepy or hysterical, the fear would be contagious. If she, as focal point of the Empire, was calm and confident, morale would remain high. The Empire would ultimately have only as much strength as she, its symbol, could project. And fortunately for the Empire, she had the inner resources to keep it strong.

But the private Edna Stanley, seen by only a privileged few, was tossed into a sea of turmoil over this revelation of possible treachery by her most trusted advisor, ally, and friend. The doubts and fears gnawed at her innards. Had she done the right thing? How secure was the Imperial Throne—and, for that matter, her very life? Who *could* be trusted if Zander turned out to be a traitor?

In a crisis like this, there was only one person with whom she could be totally at ease: her husband Liu. The Emperor-Consort was a man of quiet strength and dignity

more than a match for her own. He was a fully ordained
priest of the mystical religion of his native planet, Anares,
and a philosopher of no mean talents. Because he did not
bear the responsibility of the Empire on his shoulders, he
could be strong when she herself felt weak, and she had
drawn on that strength many times in the past.

It was not precisely love that had drawn her to him out
of her many possible suitors; love had little room in the
life of a person who would rule the Galaxy. To be sure,
love of a fashion had bloomed between them since their
meeting; she cared about him, she felt comfortable in his
presence, she knew she could depend on him to support
her in her times of need. To the extent that these factors
constituted love, then love was present. But to the extent
that love encompassed passion, it was never there. Edna
knew that, and at odd moments she felt the loss—but then
she herself was hardly what anyone would call a woman of
passions, and those moments passed quickly. She had
picked Liu as her consort because of his wisdom and his
strength, and she had never regretted her choice.

The Empress' private bedchamber was decorated to look
like the inside of a comfortable cave. The walls were
carved of volcanic rock with lush ferns growing in niches
around the room. Brightly colored silk pillows were scattered about the polished obsidian floor and the bed was a
raised platform covered by *futon* mats. Covering the back
wall behind the bed, a sisal macrame hanging held hundreds of crystal globes filled with glowing votive candles.

Alone there with Liu that evening, Edna unburdened her
troubles to him. The Emperor-Consort listened as impas-
sively as Edna had listened to the Prime Councilor earlier
that day. The Empress paced the room as she talked, her
tone becoming more uncertain as she speculated on the
consequences. "I've known Zander since I was a baby.
My father knew him and trusted him even before that. If

he wanted the throne, there are many easier ways he could have gotten it. He's third in line of succession himself now. All he'd have had to do was arrange three 'accidental' deaths—that would have been child's play for someone with his brains and resources. It doesn't make sense for him to act this way.''

"Sense is not an inherent quality of isolated facts," Liu said quietly. "Only when all things are known can the patterns be sorted out. Even then, consistency is rare." He walked over to his wife and put his hands gently around her shoulders. "When dealing with human beings, sense is the last thing anyone should expect."

"And yet I keep thinking that, in a way, it *does* make sense," Edna said with a slight sniffle. "The conspiracy knows almost everything SOTE does, and we've never been able to trace the leaks. Zander's people have filled up the holes when we've come into danger, but the margin seems to get thinner each time. At my coronation, his strategy seemed sound, but it came damned close to backfiring on us. Is he playing some subtle game? Does he enjoy moving us all around for some perverted thrill of his own?''

"I have long suspected he could play a three-dimensional chess game on a two-dimensional board," Liu said. "But capability should not be confused with actuality. If we executed everyone with a potential for outwitting us, we'd end up first on our own list."

Edna turned around and buried her face in his chest. "What can I do about this?"

"Your options are limitless. If you want to know what you *should* do, however, I suggest waiting."

"Waiting?" She gave a bitter laugh. "It seems that's all I've been doing. We've known for years that they're out there somewhere, an entire conspiracy aimed at me, and all I've been able to do is wait and see where they'll try to hit me next. They tried at our wedding, they tried at my coronation, who knows when they'll try again? Maybe I should call my father, ask his advice . . ."

"He had sixty-some years of the anxiety you have now, knowing that your Uncle Banion was somewhere out there waiting for him to slip. The six months since his abdication has been the only vacation he's ever really had. Do you feel it's proper to interrupt it with your troubles?"

Edna kissed him lightly on the neck. "You're right, as usual. The responsibility is mine now, not his. He had to live forty-five years making decisions like these. Now I have to get used to it. He may not always be around to help me; I must learn to do without a crutch." She sighed, and added, "What did you mean about waiting?"

"It seems to me that our enemy's forte is patience. He remains hidden in shadows and occasionally throws something at us to see how we react. So far, our reflexes have been excellent, and we have intercepted all his attempts. But if ever we should overreact, if we lean over too far unbalanced, I am sure our enemy will be happy to push us the rest of the way."

"Are you suggesting we do nothing? I can't take that chance. If, by some incredible misfortune, Zander really is C, I can't just let him go free. With everything he knows, he might destroy us."

"You have given much thought to the possibility of Zander's being guilty. Have you considered the alternative?"

Edna moved away from her husband and faced the macramé wall. One of Liu's greatest—and at the same time most infuriating—qualities was that he never handed her the answers she wanted. He viewed his role in her life as one of teacher, and he kept trying to make her reach for the answers herself, to stretch her mental capacity beyond the safe, normal limits. In the long run she was grateful to him for it, but at times like this, when he obviously had a suggestion, it was frustrating to have to guess at it herself.

"Of course it's something I'd like very much," she mused aloud. "But you're talking about more than my personal feelings, aren't you? *Khorosho*, let's assume Zander is innocent for a moment. What does that tell us?"

She paused and stared at the glowing candles. "It tells us," she continued, "that there is something wrong with the case against him. Either the source of the information, or the information itself—or both—is not to be trusted. Now the source is Captain Fortier; we know he's a smart, honest, and dedicated officer. He wouldn't deliberately mislead us. For the moment, I'll assume Captain Fortier is giving us the situation precisely as he sees it.

"That would leave the information itself. Fortier got it directly from the computer in Zander's own office at home. If *that's* wrong, it means the conspiracy went to great trouble to plant it there, because Zander's security is very tight. Why would they go to such trouble? Well, they know Zander is Head of SOTE, and they know I'd have to suspend him on the basis of this evidence. Without Zander, SOTE's operations will be seriously impaired, which means the conspiracy will be able to move much more freely. I see what you mean; assuming Zander's innocence leads to very interesting conclusions."

She sat down on the edge of the bed and continued to think aloud. "The trouble is, I'm caught in a fork. I can't take the chance that he's innocent, because if he isn't he can use SOTE to destroy me. But if he *is* innocent I'm needlessly taking him away from his duties and SOTE will suffer anyway. Either way, I lose. I wish I were able to consult Zander on this; he's so good at figuring a way out of such tricky situations. But I'm cut off from him, so I must do the thinking on my own."

She was quiet for a long while, staring vacantly into

space. Liu sat crosslegged on a pillow in the corner of the room, not wanting to disturb her meditation. His expression showed his confidence in his wife's abilities.

"I think I see what you meant by patience," Edna said at last. "If Zander's guilty, just holding him may force his organization to do something to free him—and they'll be the ones extending themselves for a change. If Zander's innocent, then it figures they've set him up and they'll be waiting to see how we react. If we only take minimum action, they may try to push things a little further, and again they may tip their hand." She turned and looked gratefuly at her husband. "Thank you, Liu."

The Emperor-Consort merely shrugged. "I was but the signpost. You walked the road yourself. I have learned to trust your ability to make the right decision. I hope someday you will learn to have the same faith in yourself."

"Maybe I will yet," Edna said. "After all, I've got a wonderful teacher."

Meanwhile, the instructions the Empress had given earlier that day were being carried out with the typical efficiency of the Imperial Navy. Orders were relayed from the Prime Councilor to Admiral Benevenuto; from Benevenuto to Admiral Trejas; and from Trejas all the way back to Preis and the anxiously waiting Captain Fortier, who lost no time in seeing they were carried out.

His first priority, to which he'd been attending while awaiting further orders, was to make copies of all the incriminating records and have them transmitted back to Luna Base. That task completed, he had begun interrogating the Grand Duke's house staff when the orders came in.

At this particular time, Grand Duke Zander von Wilmenhorst happened to be traveling in the Preis system. While he spent most of his life on Earth near the center of activity at the Imperial Court, von Wilmenhorst made periodic trips back to his capital to deal with government functions that could not easily be delegated to others. His private space cruiser, the *Anna Liebling,* was even now calmly approaching the planet Preis, its occupants unaware that they were at the eye of a transgalactic storm.

Captain Fortier, leading a small fleet of naval gunships, approached the *Anna Liebling* just two days after Zander von Wilmenhorst had given the assignment to the d'Alemberts and the Bavols. The order was given to the *Anna Liebling*'s Captain Hetsko to halt the cruiser's motion and permit boarders. The ship offered no resistance and Captain Fortier boarded it with a stun-gun in his holster but prepared for any trouble that might develop.

The *Anna Liebling* was a large ship, basically a giant rectangular box a hundred and twenty-five meters long by fifty meters wide and deep. It was never intended to land; there were small auxiliary boats for that which were even capable of interstellar flight in an emergency. The private ship dwarfed the naval vessels that swarmed around it; it was also better-armed than they were, though Fortier did not know that. In a fight, the *Anna Liebling* could hold its own against anything but the largest naval destroyers. But there was no such fight now. The personnel within the *Anna Liebling* followed the Navy's orders graciously.

For personal comfort, the ship's ultragrav had been set at one gee. Captain Fortier and a few of his officers were escorted down the crowded, art-lined corridors into the main salon. This was a large room of stark Scandinavian design. The sofas and chairs were of teakwood with straight, utilitarian lines, covered in blue and white tweed fabric. The walls were of glazed shades of smoke-gray. From the ceiling, as a chandelier, hung a modernistic metal sculpture of a Viking ship.

Grand Duke Zander von Wilmenhorst and his daughter, Duchess Helena, were waiting to greet the officers. The

Grand Duke was wearing a conservatively tailored gray leather jumpsuit; his daughter, an attractive young lady in her mid-twenties, had on a pair of black velvet lounging trousers and a white silk shirt. "Welcome to my ship, Captain," the Grand Duke said. "To what do I owe the honor of this visit?"

Fortier had orders to show proper deference, and he knew enough court etiquette not to embarrass the Navy. "I fear, Your Grace, I have the duty to inform you that you must consider yourself under arrest."

Duchess Helena exploded out of her chair. "What? That's utterly ridiculous! Do you know—?"

The Grand Duke raised a hand and his daughter stopped her harangue abruptly. Von Wilmenhorst looked slightly amused. "Indeed? May I ask the charge?"

"The charge, sir, is treason."

"Are you certain your orders are correct, Captain?" There was no longer amusement in von Wilmenhorst's tone.

"Yes, sir. They come directly from the Empress herself. You and Her Grace, the Duchess Helena, are to be held incommunicado until further notice."

"I see." The Grand Duke took the news philosophically. "Well, I've never known Her Majesty to act rashly, so I'll have to assume she has good reason for this, but I'd certainly like to know what it is."

"I'm empowered to explain it in detail, Your Grace," Fortier said. "But first I must ask you and your daughter to submit to searches to make sure you have no weapons on your persons. I've brought some female officers along to ensure your daughter's dignity."

"Very considerate of you, Captain," von Wilmenhorst nodded.

Duchess Helena, though, was not nearly so calm about the situation. "Father, there's got to be some mistake.

They can't mean *us*! We can't just sit here and let them do this. If we could only call her. . . ."

"The orders said incommunicado," Fortier repeated firmly.

The Grand Duke turned to face his daughter. "Just six months ago at the coronation, you and I knelt before the Empress and pledged her our allegiance and obedience in all matters. Despite the charges, I never have and never will violate that pledge. We will accede to these orders, Helena, and wait for the Empress' good judgment to assert itself."

He stood up and held his arms out to his sides. "I am ready to be searched, Captain. I hope you'll be quick about it; I'm most anxious to hear that explanation you promised."

5
Live Bait

The d'Alemberts and the Bavols spent most of the night after their discussion with the Head sitting around the large table in the com room, going over the information they'd received about the phony Wombat and Periwinkle. The doubles' method was simple and coldly efficient: They would place a call to the local SOTE headquarters, where the use of their special codenames would win them instant obedience. They'd arrange for all the agents on that world to converge at an out-of-the-way location within a very short period of time, so the local commander wouldn't have the chance to check with HQ on Earth. Once they had everyone assembled, they massacred the SOTE people without mercy—and the last place any Service agent would expect betrayal was from Wombat and Periwinkle.

"Maybe we did too good a job," Jules sighed. "We're legends in our own time, and Lady A's cashing in on that."

"How do I always get mixed up with such modest men?" Yvette wondered aloud.

"I was bragging on your behalf, too," Jules said. "But other than our codenames, the conspiracy doesn't seem to know any more about us than anyone else does. As far as we know, the doubles have never shown themselves; at least they've never left a living witness. They may be afraid their descriptions won't jibe. That may work to our advantage; if they don't know what we look like, we may be able to fool them somehow."

"Lady A certainly knows what you and I look like," Vonnie pointed out. "She got a good enough look at us on Gastonia, and since we're not listed on SOTE's regular roster, she's smart enough to figure that at least one of us is a member of the legendary team. And didn't Tanya Boros meet Yvette while you were tracking down Banion?"

"I don't think she'd remember much about me," Yvette said. "Jules was the one in the spotlight as duClos; I stayed pretty much in the background. Besides, I was heavily disguised to look middle-aged and frumpy. No, I'll bet I'm pretty much of an unknown to them—and Pias will be totally unknown."

"It looks, then," Jules said, "as though we should break up into our usual pairings. If anything requires movement on the outside, Vonnie and I will handle it since we're known anyway. You two should work behind the scenes, so we can keep your identities secret as long as possible."

"The question still remains," said Pias, "of what we are going to do to stop the slaughter of SOTE agents."

"If they keep to their pattern," Yvette said, "we know exactly when and where they'll strike. The line of their advance points straight to the planet Floreata, and the timetable they've established makes it twenty-three days from now. That gives us plenty of time to get there and plan our next move."

"But how accurately can we plan that next move?" Pias

wondered. "The impostors pick the spot of the ambush, and they only give a few hours' notice. We won't be able to work up anything too elaborate until we know the details, and then we might not have enough time."

"We also have to find a way of warning the local Service people not to fall into the trap," Vonnie said.

Pias shrugged his shoulders. "That, at least, seems simple enough. We go in there the day before and tell them what the conspiracy is doing, so they won't go to the ambush spot."

"I don't think that will work, *mon cher,*" Yvette said, shaking her head. "The impostors won't show themselves unless the SOTE squad turns up."

"Or something that *looks* like the SOTE squad," Jules murmured.

All eyes turned to him, and his sister grinned. "I recognize that expression on your face, *mon cher frère.* There are times I think even Lady A can't match you in sneakiness, and this is one of them. Would you care to share that idea with the rest of us?"

"A thought did occur to me," Jules admitted. "On Gastonia, when Lady A wanted to set an irresistable trap, she used herself as live bait, knowing we'd never pass up a chance to get our hands on her. Now she wants us; this whole scheme has been designed to draw us in. We ought to be able to use her own trick on her."

"The difference," Vonnie pointed out, "is that we wanted her alive to question her about the conspiracy. They already seem to know a lot about the Service; all she may want of us is our heads on a plate."

"I'm not so sure," Jules said. "They know a lot more about us than we know about them, that's true. But they don't know everything, or they wouldn't have set up this trap this way. I'm willing to bet they don't know *anything* about the Circus, for instance. Only a few people outside the family have ever known about it; there's been nothing in writing, nothing entered into the files. The conspiracy must know there's *something* missing from their information; we've spoiled their plans a few too many times for it to be random chance. There's something they're not taking into account, and they'll want to know what it is.

"Remember when Lady A let us capture her and inject her with what we thought was nitrobarb? She was actually criticizing us for not knowing how to operate, and for squandering such a potential resource. I think she was showing some of her true personality there—and I think if she got her hands on Agents Wombat and Periwinkle she wouldn't just kill them outright. She'd want to interrogate them to find out what pieces of the SOTE puzzle were missing. She'd be confident she could kill us later, after she found out what she needed to know."

"In other words," Vonnie said slowly, "you're proposing that *we* be the live bait in this trap."

Her husband nodded. "We'll have to take the risk. We want to go a step beyond the obvious. It's not just enough to capture or kill the impostors; the conspiracy could just start playing the game again somewhere else with a new team and we'd end up spending all our time tracking down phony Wombats and Periwinkles. We have to get behind the game and show them it won't work. They'll abandon a tactic if it proves unprofitable—we've seen that. We just have to make this damned unprofitable for them."

"I just hope the cost isn't too high for our side, too," Yvette said—and her sentiment met with no opposition from the others.

The planet Floreata was a hot world, orbiting much closer to its central star than Earth did to its primary. The polar ice caps in both hemispheres were barely noticeable, and disappeared altogether in summer. Much of the water vapor that would have otherwise condensed at the poles remained in the atmosphere, with the result that large portions of the planet's surface were perpetually overcast. The air was thick and steamy, and mists rose constantly from the top of the oceans.

There were no deserts on Floreata. Most of the planet was soggy with swampland, and warm rains were a perennial feature everywhere but the extreme northern and southern latitudes. The winds usually tended to be mild, so there were no fierce hurricanes or monsoons. There were even times when the sun broke through the cloud cover and steamed the swamps for a short while before the mists and drizzles claimed them again.

Floreata was not an easy place for humans to dwell, but people are stubborn and, once they have set their minds on living in a certain place, they will go to extremes to protect their homes. Plants of many sorts grew well in Floreata's moist heat, making the planet a rich source of agricultural products. With that as an incentive, people lived there despite the oppressive climate.

The major cities tended to be in the higher latitudes, where temperatures were more moderate by human standards. The swamps had been cleared away and enormous transparent domes had been erected to protect the cities from the worst of the rain. Little could be done about the all-pervasive humidity, however. Mildew and rotting were constant problems, and special building materials and fabrics were needed to keep civilization from falling apart after only a few years.

Despite the problems, more than six hundred million people made Floreata their home. They were dedicated and proud of their existence, and few would have moved away even if offered an alternative.

The very nature of the planet, though, offered the quartet of SOTE agents special difficulties. There were large sections of the planet still uninhabited, much of it in dismal, mucky swamps. If the impostors stayed true to form, they could set their ambush in any number of distasteful settings. "We have to let them pick the battlefield," Jules admitted during the planning sessions, "but we can provide a few surprises of our own."

Twelve hours before the impostors were due to appear, the real Agent Wombat called Service headquarters on Floreata and spoke with Colonel Josephine Reede. "We think we've located a rebel base on the far side of the fourth planet in this system. The nearest naval station of any size is a couple of days away, and by the time they could get here our birds may have flown. Can you give us a hand?"

"I'd be honored," the colonel said. "What do you need?"

"I need your entire contingent in space armor, waiting in a ship just above that planet. How many people have you got here?"

"Twelve."

"Good, that should be enough." Jules proceeded to give the colonel instructions. She and her people were to rendezvous above the fourth planet in twelve hours, and were to wait there until they received further instructions from Wombat. If they received no instructions within an additional twelve hours, it was an indication that the rebels had moved and the raid would be called off. In that event, Jules said, the SOTE people could return to Floreata with both his thanks and his apologies for bringing them on a futile mission.

Colonel Reede and her agents were destined to spend an uncomfortable half a day in space armor, keyed up for a battle that would never happen. For months afterward some of them would be griping about the experience, never knowing that they'd been taken well out of harm's way. Jules had at least made sure they'd still be alive months later to do the griping.

With all the agents out on Jules's errand, there were only a couple of civilian clerks left to mind the office. Yvette walked in with body padding and heavy makeup as a disguise and identified herself as Agent Periwinkle. The clerks, while not trained agents, knew of that codename and were dutifully obedient. Yvette explained that she would be coordinating activities on the upcoming raid, and all communications were to be channeled through her. She brought Pias in and assigned him to handle all incoming calls.

Precisely on schedule, a call came in from "Agent Wombat" demanding to speak to Colonel Reede on a matter of high priority. Pias immediately put the call through to Yvette, who had commandeered the colonel's office.

"This is Colonel Reede," Yvette said.

"This is Agent Wombat," came a voice that she knew did not belong to Jules.

"What can I do for you?" she asked, putting the proper amount of reverence in her voice.

The impostor went on to discuss plans for an attack against a criminal hideout every bit as phony as the rebel base Jules had invented. The coordinates he gave placed it, as they had feared, right in the middle of a large, unpopulated swamp. Yvette agreed to rendezvous there with all twelve of her people in two hours. The pseudo-Wombat rang off without even so much as a thank-you.

Well, Yvette thought, *Julie has lots of flaws, but at least he's more polite than that.*

Within seconds she was in contact with Jules and Vonnie,

filling them in on the details of the ambush. With that out of the way, Yvette and Pias departed, thanking the clerical staff for their help. The SOTE personnel never knew that a tragedy had just been averted.

Throughout history, every city in every civilization has had its dropouts, its losers, its hopelessly outcast. The cities of Floreata were no exception. Immediately after learning the number of agents stationed on this world, Jules and Yvonne d'Alembert had scoured the bars and slums looking for people willing to participate in their masquerade. It did not take them very long at all. It was amazing how many people were willing to play cops and robbers, no questions asked, for a hundred rubles. The agents picked ten of the cleanest they could find, who with themselves would round out the dozen.

There was barely time to arrange the transportation and fly all the phony agents to the designated spot in time for the rendezvous. Jules and Vonnie had their "team" assemble in the swamp just north of a clearing where the pseudo-Wombat had said the enemy was located. The only sign of habitation was a small plastifoam hut at the southwest corner of the clearing—hardly a job that would have required twelve agents in any case, and certainly not one that the real Wombat would have needed help on.

The d'Alemberts kept their group together and waited, swatting at the stinging insects and battling the heavy swamp stench. The ambushers were not likely to show themselves until they knew their instructions had been carried out; they knew the real Wombat and Periwinkle had probably been alerted to their tactics by now, and they would not want to make any costly mistakes.

They were not kept waiting long. A small copter appeared overhead, and the pseudo-Wombat's voice came down to Jules and Vonnie's com unit. "Glad to see you followed instructions. I want you to move in and capture the gang hiding out in that hut. Stunners only—I want them alive for questioning. My partner and I will stay up here and survey the scene, in case any of them break through your lines.''

"The hut's probably booby-trapped," Jules said, and Vonnie nodded agreement. Jules turned to their ten "confederates."

"You've served your purpose here," he told the people. "I want you to sneak off now and hide yourselves in the swamp. You can go anywhere except into that clearing, and don't go anywhere near that hut. There may be some shooting, but it won't be aimed at you. As soon as everything's settled, you can reassemble and take the copters back to the city. Thanks for your help."

The people dispersed as they were instructed, and moments later an angry call came down from the copter. "What's the matter with you? I told you to send your team into the hut, not away from it!'

"I'm operating under a different set of orders," Jules replied calmly.

"You're not Colonel Reede," the voice on the com unit accused.

"And you're not Wombat, either," Jules said. "I am."

As he spoke, he took careful aim at the copter with his blaster and fired, hoping to knock out its engine. The copter was up at the extreme range of his blaster, and the shot—though perfectly centered—did no effective damage.

The copter's occupants, realizing they were in an all-out war, immediately fired back at the two remaining figures on the ground. The craft was more heavily armed than the agents, and there was nothing ineffective about the blaster beams that came sizzling downward. Jules and Vonnie had to leap for cover into the dense vegetation as the deadly rays scorched the damp ground where they'd been standing instants before.

The copter hovered above the scene, just out of handgun range, pouring energy at a relentless intensity into the swamp where the agents had disappeared. Jules and Vonnie were not given the chance to stand and think of any cogent response to the threat. They could only move and react, trusting to their training and quick reflexes to keep them alive.

In drier terrain, the intense heat from the enemy's blasters would undoubtedly have started a forest fire, adding to the danger and confusion. The trees here were so damp that they were not about to catch fire. They sizzled under the copter's beams, emitting the powerful stench of smoldering vegetation as well as clouds of smoke and steam that helped conceal the d'Alemberts' escape.

When this initial assault failed to achieve its objective, the killers in the copter decided on a new and subtler tactic. Laying down a continuous line of blaster fire, they began moving it slowly inward toward the clearing. To the d'Alemberts, the strategy was clear: The enemy was sweeping them toward the clearing and the plastifoam hut, where they'd be perfect targets. Moving away from the clearing meant running directly into the blaster beams. They had no choice but to be pushed the way the enemy wanted them to go. Fighting against the vines that clung and tried to hold them back, they were herded closer to the clearing.

The agents did have a choice, however, about how fast they moved in that direction. The copter's passengers were taking their time about moving their sweep inward, being careful not to miss any spot where the fugitives might hide or break out of the pattern. Jules realized that if, instead of moving grudgingly toward the clearing, he and Vonnie ran through it at full speed, they might break through to the other side before the copter could re-aim.

He communicated his idea to his wife in a series of breathy orders as they ran, and she gasped her agreement. Running at top DesPlainian speed hampered by the damp springy ground and the sticky vines, they raced ahead of the blaster fire, hoping to make it through the clearing and into the underbrush beyond, where they could separate and make it harder for their foes to maneuver them.

They made it halfway through the clearing before the enemy could react. Jules had to admit that the conspiracy had picked top marksmen for this assignment; their reflexes were nearly as fast as the d'Alemberts'. Before the real SOTE agents could make it all the way across the clearing, they found that the wall of blaster fire had shifted and was now in front of them. Only their own lightning reflexes enabled them to stop in time to avoid running directly into it. Vonnie nearly fell trying to execute such an abrupt change of direction, and Jules reached out to steady her and pull her away.

The curtain of blazing energy curved about them, constricting their movements once more. They could not run back into the swamp from which they'd come, nor could they move out ahead. Their only option was toward the hut. Now that they were in the open, the enemy was able to push them faster, making them move at their most rapid pace.

It was clear that the people in the copter were toying with them; in the open like this, the d'Alemberts made easy targets for anyone with the firepower of that craft. The fact that they weren't killed outright raised Jules's hopes that his supposition was correct. The conspiracy wanted to capture him alive to find out more of what he knew. That would make what had to be done here that much easier.

Alive, though, did not necessarily mean unharmed. He

and Vonnie still could not be positive the enemy wouldn't use their blasters to incapacitate their prey.

The door to the hut stood invitingly open. They were being herded rapidly in there, even though they knew the building was booby-trapped. Their only hope lay in finding a safe way out again before the trap could be sprung.

Again they decided to use their speed as their only weapon in this situation. Outracing the wall of blaster fire behind them, they ran through the open door into the darkened interior of the hut.

The back wall of the small building was against a patch of trees, and there was a window in it. The d'Alemberts didn't need to communicate in order to coordinate their movements; there was only one option open to them. In one fluid motion they raced to the back of the hut and dived through the window back into the cover of the swamp.

Barely a millisecond behind them, the hut exploded as the blaster beams from the copter touched off a charge of explosives that had been hidden on the roof. The shock waves from the blast jarred the agents to their teeth, leaving them slightly stunned. The heat from the explosion seared their skin and pieces of debris rained down on them like a fiery hailstorm. They lay face down, unable to move from the shock for a few seconds. In those few seconds they hoped hard that the enemy did not have infrared detectors. The d'Alemberts knew they were covered by enough foliage to be invisible to the naked eye, but an infrared system would spot their body heat among the plants. The few seconds it took their nervous systems to recover from the blast left them exposed to the deadly rays from above.

But no blaster bolts came blazing down, and the SOTE agents were slowly able to pull themselves together and take further stock of the situation. Overhead they could hear the copter circling the clearing slowly, looking for any sign of human life. Seeing none, the craft spiraled warily downward so its occupants could inspect the site for themselves.

The d'Alemberts crouched and, at a whispered signal from Jules, they separated, moving to either side of the clearing, ready to attack from different angles as soon as their opponents were vulnerable. Their bodies were dripping in sweat after their exertion in the hot, damp air, but they ignored that. When d'Alemberts were on the hunt, physical discomfort meant little.

The copter touched down gently a few meters from the remnants of the exploded hut. At first, nothing happened. Then the door slowly opened and two figures emerged, a man and a woman. They were clad in lightweight battle armor—enough to deflect stunner beams and ordinary blaster bolts, yet still flexible enough to allow freedom of movement. Jules and Vonnie had their heavy-duty blasters with them, having enough power to drill right through that armor, if necessary. Each armored figure also carried a blaster. There was no polite, gentlemen's agreement, fooling around with stun weapons; these people meant business.

The pair from the copter slowly approached the remains of the hut, weapons at the ready. Jules waited until they were well away from their vehicle, making retreat impossible, and then yelled at them, "Drop your weapons. I've got a Mark Twenty-Nine Service blaster pointed at you, and it'll eat through that armor like paper."

The armored figures did not drop their weapons, nor had Jules expected them to. Even as he spoke, he was firing his own blaster. His aim was perfect; the beam struck the other man's weapon full on, reducing its components to slag almost instantly. From her hiding point across the way, Vonnie made a similar shot to disarm their other opponent.

Weaponless, now, the armored enemies were in a quandary. They could not fire back at their opponents, but there was still a slight chance they could make a break back into the copter. Jules's second shot discouraged them from considering that notion further as his beam dug a small trench between the people and their craft. Realizing they were trapped, the two killers stood still and spread their arms in a gesture of surrender.

"Strip off the armor," Jules called next, refusing to budge from his position of safety until he was sure the enemy was totally at his disposal. The two figures followed his instructions, divesting themselves slowly of the cumbersome armor until they stood revealed in the light clothing they'd worn under it.

Jules eyed them critically. They were a tough, hard-muscled pair, probably very good in a fight—but they were not DesPlainians. He'd never seen either of them before, but then he hadn't expected any old friends to show up—the conspiracy seemed to have a limitless supply of muscle to back up its plans. On a fishing expedition for Wombat and Periwinkle, Lady A would send only her best.

Only after the two traitors had fully removed their armor did the d'Alemberts step out into the clearing, guns still trained on their enemies. Stun-guns would have made the capture a lot easier, but the agents had been walking into a dangerous encounter and wanted to be certain they were armed for the worst.

They were not prepared, however, for what happened next. A loud buzzing sound filled the air, emanating from the copter, and stunner beams hit Jules and Vonnie simultaneously. There had been at least two more people hidden inside the vehicle, waiting just in case the d'Alemberts had survived the explosion.

The SOTE team dropped unconscious to the ground without even having time to appreciate the irony of the situation. Within seconds the entire outcome had been turned around, and now the d'Alemberts were prisoners of the killers who'd been impersonating them.

6
Helena Joins the Circus

Following his orders, Captain Fortier gave the von Wilmenhorsts a thorough briefing of his investigation and the conclusions that had been reached. Grand Duke Zander listened thoughtfully, occasionally interjecting a question to clarify a point in his mind. Fortier was uncomfortable in this role. He did not, of course, know that Zander von Wilmenhorst was the Head of SOTE. As far as he was concerned, the Empress had commanded him to give this explanation purely as a matter of courtesy to a nobleman of the second-highest rank in the Empire. With the evidence as convincing as it was, he also felt he was letting a powerful enemy know the details of the case against him, and he did not like that. He was duty-bound, though, to carry out the Imperial instructions.

The Grand Duke was silent for several minutes after Fortier finished the briefing. He leaned back in his chair and peered intently at a point on the floor several meters away. His mind appeared to be on another level of existence altogether, totally separate from the material universe. A hush fell over the room; Fortier knew instinctively—as Helena had learned from long experience—not to interrupt the Grand Duke when he was in a thoughtful reverie.

At last Zander von Wilmenhorst returned to the here-and-now. "Excuse me for being so distant, Captain. You've told me a fascinating tale, and the implications are truly staggering. I agree that, under the circumstances, Her Majesty had no other choice but to put my daughter and me under arrest. There are ramifications to this problem that even you don't comprehend yet, and I'm afraid I don't have the authority to enlighten you. You've done your job well, and I respect you for that."

Fortier fidgeted. According to everything he knew, the man across the room from him was the worst traitor in the Galaxy, and yet this enemy was praising him on his work. It was an uncomfortable situation, and he was leery of a trap.

"I know your orders are to hold Helena and me incommunicado," the Grand Duke continued. "I presume that means with respect to the rest of the Empire. Is there anything in your orders forbidding me from speaking privately with my daughter?"

Fortier reviewed the commands he'd been given, and had to admit there was nothing in them to prevent such communication. He'd been specifically told to treat the prisoners with the courtesy and consideration due their rank, and it seemed only fair to him that, in such time of crisis, father and daughter would want some time by themselves.

"Your privacy will certainly be respected until I have occasion to consider it a threat to the Empire," he said.

Von Wilmenhorst nodded. "Fair enough, Captain. Could you and your people please withdraw and give us a couple of minutes alone? I assure you there's only that one door to this room, and there are no communications facilities in here.''

Fortier had already scanned the room and knew that to be the truth. With a respectful bow, he and his escort left the room and closed the doors behind them as they went. Fortier posted guards on either side of the doors, with orders to notify him immediately if anything suspicious happened, then went off to report to Luna Base about the success of his mission.

Alone for the first time since their arrest, father and daughter exchanged worried glances. ''It seems we've once again underestimated Lady A,'' the Head said. ''We thought she was merely out to discredit our top agents; we didn't even think of our own vulnerability. By discrediting us, she brings into question everything SOTE's ever done since I've been in charge. Poor Edna won't know which way to turn.''

''I don't know how she can believe such a lie,'' Helena said.

''She can't afford to believe otherwise,'' her father said quietly. ''She's bent over backwards to be fair to us; we've gotten more consideration from her than anyone else would have a right to expect. She knows in her heart we're innocent, but an Empress who rules only by her heart will not be a monarch very long. She'll need hard evidence to back up what she knows.

''No, Edna's actions are not what disturb me about this affair. I have faith in her to do the right thing. What *really* bothers me is the fact that I could have had a robot traitor like Herman Stanck working as my chief assistant, governing the sector all these years, and not even realized it. I'd have sworn he was a good and honest man. It's enough to make me doubt my faith in human nature.''

''It might explain something, though,'' Helena mused.

"The conspiracy seems to know almost everything we do, and we've never been able to trace the leaks. Maybe Herman. . . ."

The Grand Duke shook his head. "No, I thought of that and discarded it. Herman's entire responsibility was to run Sector Four on my behalf. He knew nothing about my involvement with the Service—or, at least, I never told him anything. All he knew was that I spent most of my time at the court on Earth. Nothing unusual about that, most of the Grand Dukes do. Herman wouldn't have had access to even a small fraction of the information the conspiracy knows. We'll have to look elsewhere for those damnable leaks."

"And what about the subcom unit built into your security council chamber? I don't ever remember that being there. And all those files in your computer. . . ."

"We haven't been back home since just after Edna's coronation," the Head sighed. "Herman had free access to that room, and he's had months of uninterrupted time to install the subcom. Since he also had access to my computer records, he could just as easily have inserted all sorts of false, incriminating documents. There are safeguards to prevent any unauthorized information from being deleted, but it's a simple matter to insert new data into the files. I just can't get over the fact of it being Herman. I thought I knew him so well. . . ."

Helena sat up. "Maybe you did. When Fortier checked Herman's records, they showed he'd never been sick in all the time he'd been Sector Marshal. But I remember he had a lung infection a couple of years ago. I brought him flowers in the hospital. If the conspiracy can put phony data into *your* computer. . . ."

Her father nodded, a gleam in his eyes. "Yes, they can also put phony data into the personnel computer. Herman Stanck may indeed have been the trusted friend and advisor I thought he was until very recently, when they replaced him with a robot and doctored his records. In a way, I feel greatly relieved; perhaps I'm not such a bad judge of character after all. Of course, I feel dreadful about Herman; the conspiracy kills the people it replaces, and the only thing he ever did to earn a death sentence was pick the wrong man to work for. . . ."

The air hung heavy with the silence of regret. After a few moments von Wilmenhorst began speaking softly, almost to himself. "Yes, I can see how they managed to do it. They needed a brilliant and totally incorruptible man like our Captain Fortier. As with Gastonia, they had to make the case hard enough to seem as though it was not being handed over, and yet he was guided every step of the way.

"They knew he was watching Guitirrez, so they threw Helmund in his path, knowing he would eventually trace her back to Durward. They planted clues there leading him to Herman and me. They replaced Herman with a robot and altered his personnel records enough to make Fortier suspicious. The robot Herman planted false documentation in my computer and installed the new equipment in that room. He led Fortier there, displayed the proper information on the screen, and then allowed himself to be conveniently destroyed, leaving the blame on me."

The Head smiled. "Subtle and insidious, the signature of our enemy. A brilliant piece of work."

"The question is," Helena said impatiently, "what are we going to do *now?* All of SOTE is in jeopardy, and the Service may be the only thing standing between the Empire and its destruction. We've got to do something to clear our names!"

Her father spread his hands in a gesture of resignation. "There's little we can do, I'm afraid. If we were permitted even one call out, I'd contact Etienne and ask the Circus to check out these charges; if ever *their* credibility is tarnished, we might as well curl up and die. But as it is, all we can do is sit and wait and trust in Edna to do the right thing.''

Helena was staring at her father. ''You intend to just give in to this? Like a lamb being meekly led to the slaughter, without a fight?''

''I cannot and will not fight my Empress, nor disobey her orders. If I did, it would only substantiate the charges against me. The conspiracy has thought this one out very carefully, and we'll have to walk a thin line for the time being.''

''We wouldn't be fighting her, we'd be fighting the conspiracy. And we wouldn't be disobeying her orders because she never gave us any. She gave *Fortier* orders to hold us prisoner, but she never gave any commands to *us*. My oath of loyalty to her includes seeking out and destroying her enemies. That's what I want to do.''

The Head smiled. ''That's a pretty flimsy rationalization, my dear. And I don't want you running off to do anything on your own, either. You remember what happened on Sanctuary, and this time I'm in no position to send someone to rescue you.''

Helena blushed at the reference to her one attempt to engage in field work for the Service. She thought she'd been infiltrating a criminal organization, while actually she had touched on the fringes of Lady A's conspiracy. She'd gotten soon in over her head, and her father had had to send the d'Alemberts to get her out. Much was accomplished in the process and they learned of Lady A's existence for the first time, but Helena still was not proud of her failure on that case. Since then she had stuck dutifully to office work, leaving the dangerous field assignments to better qualified agents.

She said nothing further as she got up and walked out of

the room. Behind her, Zander von Wilmenhorst watched her leave, a thoughtful and unreadable expression etched on his features.

Helena was escorted to her own cabin by a young naval officer assigned to guard her. The officer remained stationed outside her door, allowing Helena the privacy and time she needed to think. She remained in her cabin for the rest of the day, having her meals sent in, while she put her plans in order.

She could understand her father's reluctance to act contrary to the Empress' wishes. He'd lived his entire life devoted to the Service code of strict obedience and loyalty to the monarch, and had brought her up according to those same principles. The sole difference was in interpretation. Her father was a man who believed in patience and gentle, constructive actions behind the scenes. Zander von Wilmenhorst was a man who preferred to watch events develop, acting only when necessary and trusting to the rashness of his opponents to make mistakes.

Helena, on the other hand, was still young enough to feel impatience with time's slow progress. She wanted things to happen *now*, and if they didn't proceed of their own accord, she was willing to push them a little.

It was all very well, she reasoned, for her father to sit calmly and hope for the best. Helena had grown up with Edna and she, too, trusted the Empress. But it was foolhardy to suppose that the conspiracy, having incapacitated the Service and thrown doubt on everything it had done, would be content to do nothing else. As Helena saw it, each day she and her father were out of commission was another day the conspiracy would use to build its own power.

She did not argue the matter with her father. She could recognize the finality in his voice, and knew that further discussion would be useless. He would not make a move counter to Edna's orders, not even to save his own life.

But Helena had to do something. From what Fortier had said, there was not a shred of evidence against her; she was only under suspicion for being her father's daughter. Perhaps Edna wouldn't think it too base of her if she ran away and tried to make some sense of this confusion. If Helena could find the truth and prove her father's and her own innocence, Edna would certainly pardon any breaches Helena made in strict observance of the Imperial commands.

She spent several hours mulling over her plan, polishing its rough edges as her father had taught her, and honing it to perfection. When her idea was well in shape, she lay back on her bed and tried to sleep for several hours. Sleep came but fitfully; she was too keyed up by the prospects of what she had to do, and true rest was impossible. After a few hours she gave up on it entirely. She changed into her favorite brown and peach-colored jumpsuit, knowing it would be sturdier for traveling. Then, gathering up her jewelry, money, and the few other possessions she thought she'd need, she put her plan into action.

Even though there was no true "night" and "day" in space, most private ships operated on specific cycles. "Day" was when most of the three hundred people aboard this ship were active, and certain functions had to be performed. "Night" was when most of the crew were sleeping, and only a few crewmen and women performed maintenance duties. It was the middle of the ship's "night" when Helena started out, ensuring the minimal opposition. As she stepped from her doorway fully clothed, the guard outside snapped to attention, hand resting close to her stun-gun.

Trying to put the guard at ease, Helena told her, "I've been thinking about this accusation of treason against my father, and I think I can *prove* he's innocent. I've got to talk with Captain Fortier. Where is he?"

"I believe he's asleep right now," the guard said with some hesitation. "Can it wait until morning?"

"I'm afraid not." Helena shook her head. "Each passing second increases the danger to the Empire. I can't even trust it over the ship's intercom. I have to speak to him in person."

"I'll have to accompany you," the other woman said.

"Of course. Where's he staying?"

"Cabin 36, Deck E."

"Fine. I know a shortcut. It'll save us going down a lot of corridors and waking people up."

The guard hesitated. This was not a situation specifically covered in her orders, but it did sound important. After a moment's indecision, she nodded and motioned for Helena to lead the way. She kept her hand near the butt of her stunner, but did not draw the weapon. The prisoner had shown no indication of hostility, and her orders were to show courtesy and use minimum force.

Helena started off at a brisk pace, and the guard had to move quickly to keep up with her. As Helena had hoped, the corridors were deserted at this time in the ship's cycle. Helena led her escort on a fast tour of the emptier parts of the ship, all the while keeping up a pleasant, innocuous conversation indicating she was resigned to her captivity. The officer was a little out of breath and just enough off guard by the time they reached the spot Helena had chosen to make her move.

There was one place where, due to a design problem, the hallway made a slight S-bend. As she reached it, Helena turned and abruptly slowed her rapid pace. The officer, who'd been walking quickly to keep up, did not slow quite as fast and almost bumped right into Helena.

Helena gave a slight laugh and said, "Excuse me," then reached out as though to steady the officer.

In a quick gesture, she pushed the other woman hard against the bulkhead and snatched at the stun-gun in her holster. The officer, realizing belatedly that she'd been tricked, tried to grab Helena by the collar, but the SOTE woman ducked under the outstretched hand and pulled the stunner free. Before the guard had a chance to do more than utter a startled cry, Helena had shot her with the weapon and the woman sagged to the deck.

Helena checked the setting on the stunner and saw, much to her relief, that it was set on three—a half-hour stun. The guard would wake up in a short while greatly embarrassed, but otherwise none the worse for her failure. Helena had been worried that the stun-gun might be set so high as to cause real damage—but the orders to use minimum force were being carried out accurately. Helena did not want to harm anyone on her own side who just happened to be in the awkward position between her and her freedom.

She looked around, but there appeared to be no one who'd heard the brief cry; this part of the ship should be well deserted at this hour, which was one reason Helena had chosen it. Another reason was that it was near the emergency escape boats that were her next destination.

As the private space yacht of a Grand Duke, the *Anna Liebling* would naturally have been an impressive craft. But with its owner also being the Head of the Service of the Empire, it was equipped very well indeed. Not only could it hold its own in a military battle, but its emergency craft had subspace capabilities, a rare commodity. The boats were not the fastest in the Empire, perhaps—but with a little luck and a good headstart, Helena felt sure she could outrace anything Fortier currently had available to him. By the time he could call up anything faster, she hoped to be off his screens and too far gone to catch.

She slid like a ghost through the silent halls, stun-gun at the ready, alert for the slightest sign of trouble. She encountered no one until just before she reached the emergency airlocks, where Fortier had stationed a couple of his men. Helena stunned them both before they had a chance to draw their own weapons, then moved to the bank of lockers beside the pressure doors. She was never more glad that her father had ordered a spacesuit specifically tailored to everyone who normally traveled aboard this ship.

All shuttlecraft that went to and from the *Anna Liebling* docked in a hangar open to the vacuum of space. Normally, boarding tubes snaked out to connect up with the airlocks of the ships, allowing visitors to come aboard without having to don the cumbersome spacesuits. But sending out a boarding tube was a function controlled from the *Anna Liebling*'s bridge, and under the circumstances Helena could not afford to be that formal.

Instead, she would have to put on her own spacesuit and go out the airlock, then board the emergency craft in a manual mode. Even this was a calculated risk, for the opening of the emergency airlock would cause a light to flash on the control board. The emergency hatch had a manual operating mode and could not be overridden from the bridge, which was a point in her favor; but once she started the process, a clock would be ticking for her. Everything then would depend on how quickly the alarm was noticed and how decisively her captors acted on it. She was hoping there would at least be a few minutes of initial confusion, giving her time to get through the hatch, enter one of the lifeboats, and blast out of the *Anna Liebling* before anyone really knew what was happening.

She donned the suit carefully, checking all the joints and

seals as she'd been trained to do. Then, after staring at the
doorway for a few nervous seconds and offering up a silent
prayer, she pressed the emergency exit plate beside the
hatch.

The portal slid aside quickly with a clang Helena could
hear even through her helmet. Stepping inside, she pressed
the inner plate to close the hatch again and open the outer
chamber door. Normally this would have been a slow
process, with the outer door not opening until all the air
had been pumped out of the lock; but the emergency
airlock had been designed for quick use, and the small
amount of air that would be lost to space was considered
trivial when people needed to get out of the ship in a
hurry.

As the outer door opened, Helena rushed toward the
nearest escape boat. She had to assume the emergency
light had been seen on the bridge the instant she opened
the hatch, and that steps would be taken instantly to recapture her. She had few seconds to spare.

The emergency boats of the *Anna Liebling* were always
kept in prime condition, and the one she'd chosen re-
sponded instantly to her command. Without even bothering to remove her helmet, Helena slipped into the pilot's
seat and brought the control console to life with a quick
flip of the necessary switches. The engines charged up and,
with a sudden acceleration that shoved her hard against
her couch, the boat shot out of its berth and into the
blackness of space.

The *Anna Liebling* was surrounded by a swarm of small
craft like fireflies, the escort Captain Fortier had brought
with him to ensure there'd be no trouble. As Helena's craft
zoomed from the big ship's hangar, her radio crackled to
life with a challenge to halt. Helena ignored the request,
which quickly turned into a cold, hard order. She flew at

three-quarters speed, hoping the Navy ships would be tricked into thinking that was as fast as she could go.

A warning shot blazed across her path, but Helena flew straight on. She made no attempt to dodge or weave her way through a field of fire; any motion other than straight forward would only slow her down. She had to trust to the accuracy of the naval gunners, and to the fact that they'd been ordered to use minimal force to capture and hold her. They'd be reluctant to simply blow her out of the sky, and would try to disable her instead.

The screens showed that four ships had left their positions around the *Anna Liebling* and had come in pursuit. They were gunboats of the *malyenki* class—not much firepower, but plenty of speed and maneuverability. Helena's boat probably had as much armament as they did, but she didn't want a fight.

She'd had perhaps a thirty-second headstart, but the gunboats were slowly gaining on her. Helena watched them carefully on her screen, judging their distance and speed in relation to hers, and suddenly boosted her own vessel to maximum acceleration. On the screen, the images of the Navy ships seemed to jump backwards to the limit of detection range. At almost the same instant, Helena, hoping to catch her pursuers unaware, had her craft make the jump into subspace.

The trick worked to perfection. The gunboats, confident they could outrun the fugitive, were unprepared for its sudden burst of acceleration. Their commanders were just making the adjustments for the new speed when the vessel disappeared into subspace—something ordinary lifecraft were incapable of. By the time they could adjust to this second surprise and switch into subspace themselves, Helena's boat was totally off their screens. They split up and fanned out in different directions for a short while, hoping to pick up some trace of her, but they were out of luck.

Red-faced, the officers returned to their positions around the *Anna Liebling*, wondering how to explain to Captain Fortier that a small emergency craft had outraced and outmaneuvered four Imperial gunboats.

Helena managed to elude capture by staying in subspace for only about ten seconds, then dropping into normal space again and killing all acceleration completely. Ten seconds in subspace let her travel far enough to be out of range of normal detection systems; her boat would appear merely as a floating piece of space rock to any casual observer. And by dropping out of subspace before the Navy vessels could enter it, their subspace detectors would not spot her, either.

She spent a tense three hours watching her own screens nervously, in case Fortier caught on to her trick. When at last she was convinced she'd gotten away undetected, she began cruising—at slow, deliberate speed—back toward the planet Preis. The Navy would send out warnings to all planets for a large radius around, but she hoped they would be a little less alert within the system she had supposedly escaped from.

Even so, she was careful not to land at a spaceport. She brought her lifeboat down well away from any populated centers and spent two days walking back into the nearest town. With the money she had at hand, she bought a tube ticket to the capital city of Aachen. Two days of walking through semi-wilderness had left her face tanned and weatherworn enough to be unrecognizable to the people who normally knew her as the heir to this sector. A few subtle makeup tricks she'd learned at the Service Academy completed the job.

In Aachen she sold some of the jewelry she'd brought with her. She hated to part with some of her favorite pieces, but the situation was desperate. The money she got for the jewelry was enough to buy her some more clothes and a spaceliner ticket to the planet Evanoe, where the Circus of the Galaxy was currently performing.

The Circus of the Galaxy was one of the prime entertainment events throughout the Empire, a show offering more live thrills and excitement than even the wildest sensible adventure could match. More than that, though, the Circus was one of the primary weapons in SOTE's formidable arsenal because it was the personal business of the d'Alembert family. All of its performers, all of its staff—nearly a thousand people—were members of that impressive clan from high-gravity DesPlaines. The d'Alemberts were noted for both their incredible talents and their fierce dedication to the Imperial Throne. Whenever there was a difficult and sensitive task, the Service naturally turned to the d'Alemberts to perform it. Now, in her moment of greatest need, Helena also wanted to call on the Circus.

The flight from Preis to Evanoe took a full week. Helena fretted the whole time. She knew that both the Service and the Navy would be looking for her, and that all sorts of things might be happening in the silent, secret war between the Empire and the conspiracy. Aboard a liner in subspace she was perfectly safe from outside intrusion, but at the same time she was effectively out of touch with any developments that might occur. As her father's chief aide, she'd spent the last few years being in constant contact with developments all over the Galaxy; now she was suddenly cut off from all news, and the silence was deafening.

She wasted no time upon landing, but took a tube train straight to the area where the Circus had set up its camp. It was late at night when she arrived, long after the last performance of the day. All the customers had gone, the midway was shutting down, the normally hectic atmosphere was subdued. The smell of strange animals mingled oddly with the odors of foods from a thousand different worlds. Helena slipped quietly onto the grounds and, trying not to let anyone see her, made her way to the main office.

Because the Circus was traveling most of the time, its personnel tried to make their surroundings as homey as possible. The main office was thickly carpeted in turquoise blue and the walls were paneled in richly-grained solenta-wood. Three sides of the room were lined with book-shelves. Antique books were both a hobby and an obses-sion with Duke Etienne, who insisted that bookreels just didn't feel right. Some of the volumes in his collection were more than five hundred years old.

Etienne d'Alembert, Duke of DesPlaines and Managing Director of the Circus of the Galaxy, was sitting behind his new bronze burlwood desk, and looked up as Helena entered. The duke was a short, somewhat portly man of about fifty, his hair graying at the temples and thinning in front—but his innocuous appearance disguised a person of incredible power and ability. Rumor was that Etienne was the only man who'd ever beat Helena's father at chess; he'd been as close to Helena as any uncle, even though they seldom actually saw one another.

"The perimeter guards spotted you and let me know you were coming," he said quietly. His eyes were filled with sadness as looked at her now. "I turned off the ultragrav in here so you'd be comfortable. I wish I could say this visit was a surprise."

Helena nodded. "They told you, I suppose, that I might try to contact you."

"Yes. I have orders from Edna herself to take you into custody if you showed up here."

Helena's entire body was trembling; she was very close to tears. "Please, Etienne," she said, her voice barely more than a whisper. "My father and I need you."

The Duke's left hand clenched, and he stared silently at the woman before him for almost a minute before he replied. "You haven't heard, then?"

"Heard what?" Helena could scarcely choke the words out of her mouth, it was so dry with horrible premonition.

"Oh, my poor girl. Your father was executed two days ago on a charge of treason."

7
_____ Revelation _____

The killers impersonating Agents Wombat and Periwinkle
carried the unconscious bodies of Jules and Yvonne
d'Alembert to their waiting copter, where their confederates helped them stow the SOTE agents away in the back
cargo section. The DesPlainians had been given a number
four stun, and would be unconscious for at least two
hours, which would give the killers plenty of time to take
them to more secure quarters.

Several kilometers away, Pias and Yvette were monitoring events as they happened. Knowing they'd be
walking into a trap and assuming they'd be captured,
Jules and Vonnie had planted microtransmitters on their
clothes and bodies. These devices enabled the Bavols
to follow the action—at least what could be heard of it—
from a safe distance, and to trail after the killers without coming close enough to be spotted themselves. "We
want to make sure we get the whole gang at once," Jules
had said. "With Vonnie and me as bait on the hook, we'll

give them a little play on the line before reeling them in.''

Yvette was not happy with the thought of standing idly by and listening to her brother and sister-in-law be captured by the enemy—but, like her brother, she wanted to grab the whole gang in one sweep. If they acted too quickly, some might escape to spread the warning further up the network. This move had obviously been planned by someone higher up within the conspiracy; a little patience might lead them to big game indeed.

The Bavols listened to the confused mixture of sounds that were the obvious indications of a battle in progress. The buzzing sound of stun-guns was ominous, because neither Jules nor Yvonne had carried stunners into the battle. The silence that followed made it only too clear that the enemy had gained the upper hand. Even though this was part of their long-term plan, Yvette's fists were clenched in quiet anger.

As the killers' copter left the clearing, the Bavols' vehicle rose into the air and followed. The signals broadcast by the microtransmitters were strong enough for the agents to stay far behind their prey, out of both visual and normal detector range. The two copters flew at a steady, casual pace toward the nearest domed city, Constantia.

The enemy copter landed on the rooftop parking lot of an apartment building. The Bavols made a note of the site and flew on to a nearby perch. They listened and waited. That was the hard part—the waiting.

Within the target building, the enemy agents had rented an entire floor for themselves. After searching their captives for weapons—but missing the transmitters, which looked like ordinary buttons—they handcuffed the d'Alemberts' hands behind their backs and went about their normal business until the two superagents recovered from the stun they'd received.

After a while, Jules started coming around. Reality weaved in and out of focus for him and his surroundings gradually became more distinct. When he could recall what had happened, he looked around him. He was in a bedroom, but his body had been dumped on the floor. Vonnie lay on the floor across the room from him, still unconscious; stun-guns had slightly differing effects on different people's nervous systems, and Vonnie was apparently more susceptible. Jules was not going to worry about her yet.

As Jules looked around further, he could see someone sitting on the bed watching him: the woman who'd come out of the copter. She eyed him coolly for a moment, then called into the next room, "The man's come to."

A man came into the room—not the one Jules had seen in the clearing. This must have been one of the people waiting in the copter to complete the ambush. It scarcely mattered; this man looked every bit as competent as the one Jules had seen.

The man knelt beside Jules and checked for any residual traces of shock from the stunner. When he was satisfied Jules was all right, he turned to the woman and said, "Call the battlestation. I think he's ready to talk now."

The woman went into another room and Jules, by straining, could just make out the sounds of a subetheric communicator being adjusted. There was a muffled dialog he couldn't quite hear, and then the woman returned. "She's ready for him."

The man grabbed Jules roughly by the shirtfront and pulled him to his feet. "In there, Wombat," he sneered, giving Jules a hard shove in the general direction of the adjoining room. Jules's legs were still a little wobbly from the after-effects of the stun. He staggered a bit, provoking laughs from the two killers.

"Some superagent," the woman taunted. "He can't even walk straight."

With monumental effort, Jules fought to recover his balance and walked with dignity through the doorway into the next room. His action did not stop the jeering of the traitors, but it at least satisfied his own sense of honor. Another woman he hadn't seen was standing beside a portable subcom set. In the set's triscreen was the three-dimensional image of someone Jules had seen and worked against before: Tanya Boros, erstwhile Duchess of Swingleton and daughter of Banion the Bastard.

She obviously recognized him, too, because her eyes narrowed slightly and her face took on a colder expression. "Well, well," she said. "Who are you supposed to be this month? Shall I call you duClos or Brecht?"

"I think today I'll be René Descartes," Jules retorted. His tongue felt thick and heavy as an aftereffect of the stun, and it slurred his speech a little more than he'd have liked. He hated showing any weakness in front of this proud, beautiful woman.

Boros did not like his impudent answer. Rage flashed momentarily across her face. Her temper was always her weak point, Jules knew, but now she was making some effort to moderate it. After a brief struggle she returned her expression to one of bland superiority. "I think I'll just call you Wombat for now," she said. "From what I've been told it's a rather ugly, awkward animal—quite fitting for someone like you."

"Is that why you tried to seduce me several years ago?"

Boros refused to be baited. "I was bored and looking for new perversions. Believe me, you'll never get an offer that generous again in your lifetime. And if you want that lifetime extended to any degree, you'll cooperate and answer a few questions."

"I never deal with the hired help."

"Oh, you can ignore those people holding you prisoner. I'll do the interrogation."

"That's just who I meant. You're not important enough for me to deal with. Lady A's running this show, so she can question me herself."

Once again he'd touched off a spark of anger in the young woman. "Do you think she has time to drop everything for a *kulyak* like you? I'm in charge of this operation, and you'll do what I tell you. I'm going to get information out of you. I can get it painfully or pleasantly, the choice is entirely your own."

"How can I respect someone who won't even face me in person?"

"Why should I take the risk? I'm safe in my battlestation. You've never told me the truth when we've met in person before, so I have nothing to lose by remaining where I am. My surrogates there will administer all the persuasion you require; my only regret is that I won't be able to do to you myself what needs to be done. They'll call me back when you're loosened up a bit." Her image reached out to touch an unseen control, and the screen went blank.

Jules had gotten far more information than he'd given in that conversation. He now knew the extent of this impersonation scheme: Tanya Boros in charge and these four blasterbats carrying out her instructions. A small but efficient operation. Boros herself was safely ensconced in something she called a battlestation, and was not about to be lured out of it. He had accomplished all that could be accomplished from this position. It was now time to get himself and Vonnie rescued.

The woman beside the subcom set had a truncheon in her hand and was slapping it gently against her other palm. She eyed Jules with a sadistic gleam. "We drew lots to see who'd question you first," she said. "I won."

"Surely there must be some alternative," Jules said.

"You could tell me all about yourself. If I believe you, I *might* go easy."

"*Khorosho*. I was born in a little log cabin. My parents died when I was three, and I was raised in the wild by a pack of wolves. . . ."

Wham! The truncheon hit him in the diaphragm, and Jules doubled over, gasping for breath. "One thing you'll find," the woman said, grabbing him by the hair and forcing him to look directly into her face, "is that my friends and I have strange senses of humor. Instead of laughing when we hear a joke, our reaction is to inflict pain. The funnier the joke, the more pain we give."

"Remind me, then, not to tell you the one about the spaceman's daughter and the model rocket builder," Jules gasped.

This time the woman used the weapon to jab Jules hard in the kidneys. The DesPlainian doubled over in pain, and another sharp blow to his back made him fall to his knees. As he regained his breath he tilted his head to look up at the woman standing over him. "I guess you must have heard that one before."

There followed a series of blows beyond counting. Jules's body was bloody and battered by the time the woman was finished. Blood was dripping from his nose and mouth, and he could not have done much talking even if he'd wanted to. The woman realized this, too, for she snarled at him as she pushed him back into the bedroom; her fun was over for a while. She looked at Vonnie, but the female agent was still unconscious from the stun-gun beam, so Jules and his wife were left alone in their little room.

Jules gave some thought to the conditions of his bondage. Though his wrists were handcuffed firmly behind him, there was a little bit of play between the two bracelets. His second cousin Alphonse, the contortionist, had taught him some of the secrets of that trade—enough so that, with some squirming about on the floor, Jules was able to work his bound arms down below his buttocks, along his legs, and past his feet. His arms were still handcuffed, but now his hands were in front of him, giving him far more freedom of movement. His Uncle Marcel, the Circus' magician, could have gotten out of the handcuffs altogether—probably by using a picklock hidden somewhere on his body—but Jules had never learned that stunt. This amount of freedom would have to do for now.

He was more concerned about Vonnie. His wife was still showing no sign of coming out of the stun, and that was a bit alarming. She'd been shot by a different gun than the one that had hit him; could it have been adjusted to a different setting, one that had a longer or—he hated to consider the possibility—a permanent effect? The killers wouldn't have brought her here if she'd been dead, but a setting of eight or nine would have her unconscious for days and perhaps leave permanent paralysis when the charge wore off. That was too horrifying to even consider, so he turned his thoughts to more immediate matters.

Things should be happening very shortly, he knew. He and the Bavols had established the word "alternative" as a code phrase indicating they were to come in and rescue the captives. He had no doubt that his sister and brother-in-law were monitoring the conversations, and they would have set out the instant they heard him say that word to the woman questioning him. That had been ten or fifteen minutes ago; they were probably scouting this hideout for the best entrance. They'd be here very shortly and, despite the pain from his beating, he wanted to be in as good a position as possible to help them out.

Jules's assumptions were correct. The moment Yvette and Pias heard him say to his interrogator, "Surely there must be some alternative," they went into action. That signal meant Jules had decided he'd gotten all he could from the situation; now it was up to them to disentangle him from it.

According to the directional antenna on their receiver, Jules and Yvonne were being held captive on the fourth floor down from the top in the apartment building. It took the Bavols just a few minutes to fly their own copter to the landing pad on the roof, after which they had to spend some time surveying the situation.

An elevator tube led down from the roof into the building. The door to the tube was locked—probably only residents were given keys—but that was no problem to someone with Yvette's skills at burglary. She had the door open in under a minute. It was the elevator tube itself that offered unexpected difficulties.

"The plates won't even stop on the floor we want unless we've got a special access number," she explained to Pias after examining the setup. "And the doors won't open at that level without the plate stopping there."

"There must be some other way in, then," her husband said. "We've got enough line with us; we could lower ourselves over the roof and swing down into that level through the windows."

Yvette shook her head. "We can do it that way if there's no other choice, but I don't want to be that blatant. The crashing of glass would alert everyone in the building, and the police might get involved. Let's see if we can figure out something else."

After looking down the elevator tube for a little while longer, they came up with a workable plan. There was a series of handholds down the sides of the tube, giving ready access to maintenance personnel. They climbed down the dusty rungs into the darkness of the tube until they reached the doors that opened onto the level where the impostors were holding Jules and Yvonne. Now the only problem was to get the doors open.

Whatever method was used, it would have to be quick. The killers knew that no one but them should have the access numbers for this level. If anyone else came out of the elevator tube, they'd shoot first and ask questions later.

There was a small nodule of electrical connections beside the doorway. Yvette studied the configuration for a moment, then reached down to a compartment in her belt and took out a wad of explosive. After rubbing it between thumb and forefinger for a moment to bring it to body temperature, she stuck it onto the connections and attached a short fuse. She and Pias drew their stun-guns and braced themselves as best they could in their awkward footholds against the naked wall of the elevator tube.

The fuse sputtered, and there was a small *puff* as Yvette's charge blew the doors' controlling circuits. The doors slid quickly into the wall and the two agents clambered awkwardly through the opening. For an instant they were easy targets.

Their attack caught the killers completely off guard. Boros's minions, expecting no trouble, did not have their guns at their sides, and were not prepared to fight back against the Bavols' furious invading force. The SOTE team need not have worried; with their reflexes and weapons already drawn, the battle was over in a matter of seconds.

The sound of action brought Jules stumbling out of the back bedroom just as Pias and Yvette were finishing their work. Yvette was horrified to see how badly her brother had been beaten, but Jules quickly reassured her. "I'm smooth. Just get these off me." He held up his hands to indicate the cuffs that bound his wrists.

They searched through the killers' pockets until they found the key and freed Jules. Then, while Pias took care of securing the prisoners before they woke up, Yvette went into the back room with Jules to tend to Vonnie.

She was just starting to come around as they entered the room, and Jules was immeasurably relieved. He cradled his wife while Yvette unlocked the manacles, and Vonnie slowly regained her strength. She could see from the fact that Yvette was also there that the rescue operation had already been accomplished. "Looks like I missed the fun," she said weakly. Then, seeing Jules's bloody face, she said, "Are you all right, *mon cher*?"

"Smooth," Jules assured her. "I've had massages rougher than that. I'm more worried about you; you took far too long coming out of stun."

"Different people come out at different speeds," Vonnie said.

"But you've been stunned before and it's never taken you this long to come out of it."

Vonnie and Yvette exchanged knowing glances, and Vonnie looked away, embarrassed. It was up to Yvette to give the explanation. "She's never been pregnant before, either."

"Pregnant!" For a moment, Jules felt almost as though he'd been hit by another stun-beam. His face broadened in a silly, toothy grin. "How long . . . oh, darling! Why didn't you tell me before?"

"I just found out the day you and Pias went on that training flight through the asteroids," Vonnie answered sheepishly. "I was going to tell you that night, but then the Head called and it didn't seem like the right time."

Jules's face grew serious again as a dark thought crossed his mind. "You should never have come on this assignment," he said accusingly. "It's far too dangerous."

"Don't go protectionist on me all of a sudden," Vonnie said. "It was far more dangerous on Gastonia or Slag than it is here. You didn't worry about me then. I can still take care of myself.''

''But it's not just you I'm worried about; there's also the baby to consider. Sure, you can still take on an army of blasterbats, but what if an accident happens? You just suffered a stun-gun charge. How will that affect the baby? How do we know it won't happen again, or worse? We've got to think about the future now and take a few precautions.''

''I can handle myself,'' Vonnie insisted.

Yevette felt it was time for her to speak up. ''Jules is right, Vonnie,'' she said soothingly. ''You have as much responsibility towards seeing that there's a new generation of d'Alemberts as you do towards solving this particular case. Jules and Pias and I can handle this job without you, but *you're* the only one who can have that baby.''

''But I'll feel so useless knowing you're all risking your lives and I'm doing nothing.''

''You won't be idle,'' Jules assured her. ''We've got four prisoners. I don't think we should turn them over to the police just yet; that would alert the conspiracy that we've captured their people and we might lose our connection with Tanya Boros.'' Jules went on to explain to his wife what had happened since their capture, including the fact that his old nemesis was in charge of this operation.

''If Boros knows we've captured her *mokoes*,'' he concluded, ''she might decide to go back to her headquarters. Until we can pry her out of this 'battlestation' she's got, we need someone to keep an eye on the prisoners. It's not an exciting job, but it *is* important.''

Yvonne grumbled a bit, but she was practical enough to see the sense in what Jules had said. She let her husband help her to her feet and the three SOTE agents went back out into the front rooms, where Pias had finished locking up the prisoners in their own handcuffs.

The job of interrogating the captives fell to Yvette, since she'd had special training in that delicate art. She didn't expect the killers to be very cooperative, but she'd come prepared with chemical inducements. Realizing that the prisoners were not of a high enough level to resist the questioning, she didn't bother with nitrobarb; detrazine would be good enough to extract all the information she needed.

As it turned out, the four killers knew surprisingly little. They were not really members of the conspiracy at all, just a team of hired assassins chosen to participate in this particular operation. They knew nothing about the conspiracy's organization; their only contact was through Tanya Boros, who stayed secluded on her battlestation and directed their efforts over the subcom. One of the killers did know the battlestation's coordinates; it was drifting in interstellar space less than a parsec away from Floreata.

Their next move seemed clear. They would have to drop by this battlestation and pay a visit to Tanya Boros. Perhaps she would be able to lead them higher up the conspiracy's ladder, to Lady A and C themselves.

8
_____ *Durward Again* _____

Etienne d'Alembert's announcement of her father's execution hit Helena like an avalanche. There was suddenly a cold, hollow place in her stomach, and her very being seemed to be draining out a hole. Her head was shaking automatically in denial, and her body felt as though it were made of wet snow. Her knees began to sink slowly, no longer able to support the weight of her body.

Etienne d'Alembert, seeing Helena in shock, rushed from behind his desk to embrace her and guide her to an armchair. Helena's body felt clammy to his touch; there was a cold sweat breaking out on her forehead. A fit of shivering gripped her, and he held her tightly until the seizure subsided. Even so, her teeth were chattering so convulsively she could not talk.

Duke Etienne went to his intercom and called to the commissary for a large pot of hot chocolate. By the time it arrived, Helena was beginning to look herself again. She gratefully accepted the cup of chocolate Etienne poured her.

"I . . . I didn't think she'd . . . how . . . what were the details?" she stammered around sips of the drink.

The Duke sighed, sitting on the edge of his desk and watching the young woman's face intently. "There weren't many details released to the public at all. The newsrolls merely said that Grand Duke Zander von Wilmenhorst had been seized and charged with high treason. Because the nature of the crime was so sensitive, he was taken back to Earth and summarily executed."

"Without even a trial?" Helena asked. "A Grand Duke deserves at least a High Court of Justice. Even Banion got one of those."

Etienne shook his head sadly. "The Empress has, of course, the authority to do anything she pleases. A High Court of Justice is customary and traditional in such cases, but the Empress overruled that tradition. In view of your father's sensitive position, I can hardly blame her for wanting to keep everything secret. By the way, nothing whatsoever was said in the newsrolls about you; it's as if you didn't exist."

Helena blinked uncomprehendingly. "But what about Sector Four? That should be mine now."

"I'm afraid not. Because of the nature of the crime, the Empress took back governance of the sector, and is said to be studying who to appoint as the next Grand Duke or Duchess. You've been disinherited."

Shock upon shock. Helena had been raised all her life with the certain knowledge that one day she would be the ruler of Sector Four, one of the richest women in the Galaxy, with power rivaled by few and inferior only to the Empress herself. Suddenly, in one swift stroke, all of that was gone. She no longer even had the right to claim her noble title. She was just plain Helena von Wilmenhorst, presently unemployed and fleeing from Imperial justice.

She sat in silence for a few moments, sipping at her

chocolate as the heavy news sank in. "I . . . I can't believe. . . ."

"I also received a private call from Edna herself," Etienne added when it was clear Helena would not finish her sentence. "She broke the news to me personally, before I could hear it from anywhere else. She told me a bit of what had happened—that there was some evidence that your father was this notorious C who ran the conspiracy."

"All fradulent," Helena said, her voice barely more than a whisper.

"She said she had trouble believing it herself," the Duke continued. "She wanted to keep both of you under simple house arrest at first—but when you escaped, she realized that couldn't work. She had your father brought back to Earth and executed secretly before anything more could happen. She was almost in tears as she told it to me."

"*Bozhe moi,*" Helena said, her lower lip trembling. "I killed him. He told me it might make us look more guilty, but I ignored him. If I hadn't run away. . . ."

That was as far as she could get before her grief and guilt overwhelmed her. Her eyes filled with tears; her body convulsed with heavy sobbing. She leaned forward in her chair, dropping the cup of chocolate to the carpeted floor, and wrapped her arms tightly around her knees. Her head was bowed, and for several minutes the only sounds in the room were her small gasping noises and whimpers of utter misery. Etienne watched her dry-eyed. He'd done his crying two days ago; he had no tears left now.

When Helena seemed to be coming back under control, he offered her his handkerchief to dry her eyes and wipe her running nose. "Edna and I also talked about you," he said quietly.

Helena looked up at him, eyes and nose both bright red. "Oh?"

"Yes. I promised her that if you came here, I would take you into my custody, and that the Circus would not be used to help you with any private missions to clear your father's name."

Helena had thought her heart could sink no lower, but now found there were new depths to her despair. The Circus had been her one last hope to find justice, and even that was to be denied her. The whole universe was empty, and all about her was darkness. "You might as well just shoot me now," she said mechanically. "I have nothing more to live for."

"Before you submerge yourself completely in self-pity, there are a few things *I'd* like to know," Etienne said in an even tone. "Her Majesty didn't have time to give me a full briefing on the case, and I'm still very puzzled. Your father was the dearest friend I had in this life, and if he was condemned to death I'd like to know the reason. Do you know anything more about the charges?"

Slowly, mechanically, Helena recited the story of Fortier's investigation as the captain had told it to her. She knew it by heart, having gone over and over it on the trip from Preis hoping to find some flaw in its logic. She spoke in a near-monotone; she was numb, and all emotion had fled from her body.

Etienne d'Alembert paced around the room as he listened. His vibrant energy could hardly have been less like the studied calmness her father had affected when receiving a briefing, but there was an intensity of concentration and thought that recalled her father very much. The slight similarity caused a minor ache in Helena's soul, but with so much grief already present she scarcely noticed.

When she finished, the Duke was shaking his head vehemently. "That's not enough," he muttered. "I wouldn't condemn a flea on evidence like that. Why did she do it? I don't understand. *Eh bien*, she *is* the Empress. . . ." He fell silent and resumed pacing. Helena sat silently, waiting for him because she had nothing else to do.

At last he stopped pacing and looked squarely at Helena. "*Khorosho*, let's look at Fortier's story. It breaks into three parts, on three different planets: Lateesta, Durward, and Preis. Everything that happened on Lateesta was perfectly straightforward, and everything on Preis was neatly wrapped up when the robot ran into your father's house and conveniently opened up his files. But Durward remains unfinished business; Elsa Helmund got away, and nobody pursued that connection any further. If there's any weak point to the story at all, it's there."

He paused to roll the name around in his mind. "Durward." The very name conjured up long and unpleasant memories, dating back to a time even before Etienne had been born. Durward had been a source of uneasiness within the Empire for more than sixty years, entangling and killing many fine SOTE agents in its web of intrigue.

It began when Emperor Stanley Nine was on the throne. Duke Henry Blount of Durward, in an effort to consolidate more power for himself, arranged for a beautiful and unprincipled young actress named Aimée Amorat to become the Emperor's mistress. Amorat—later to be known as the "Beast of Durward"—had a son by the Emperor, and the child was officially acknowledged as heir to the throne. For form's sake, Amorat was married to Duke Henry, but her influence over the Emperor continued—until he was presented with a *legitimate* heir by his wife. The older child, Banion the Bastard, was now far more than an embarrassment; he was a threat to the orderly Imperial line of succession.

Having led an unsuccessful rebellion against her husband Henry, Aimée Amorat took her son and vanished just a step ahead of SOTE. For over sixty years SOTE had searched in vain for that child and the royal patent he'd been issued; not until just a few years ago, when it was almost too late, had Jules and Yvette tracked down Banion and smashed the organization he'd built over the years. Even Banion did not know what had become of his mother, but it was assumed she was either dead or infirm by now, since she'd be a woman in her middle nineties.

In the meantime, the very name Durward raised uncomfortable feelings in any SOTE agent. The Banion case was closed, but bad memories lingered like the smell of old garbage.

Duke Etienne stroked his right hand as he thought, and anyone who knew him well would recognize that as an important sign. The Duke's right hand had been severed by a blaster bolt during the course of one mission, and was now replaced by a very real-looking artificial one. The detachable fingers were tools and implements of various sorts; the Duke wore rings on each finger to disguise the seams where the fingers joined to the hand.

Duke Etienne looked back at Helena. The young woman was staring emptily into space, still in shock from the horrible news she'd received. "Your father was the closest friend I had," Etienne told her. "I can't believe he was guilty as charged. Something in Captain Fortier's story is itching at the back of my brain, and I won't feel right until I investigate the matter personally."

"But you promised Edna you wouldn't," Helena said lifelessly.

Etienne gave her an encouraging smile. "I promised I wouldn't use the Circus to help *you*. But this is something I want to do for myself. Unless I'm given a specific assignment that takes priority, I've always been free to follow my own course to help Imperial security. Right now, there's nothing more important to me than finding the truth about your father.''

He stood up, walked to her side, and lifted her chin so she was looking straight into his eyes. "I also promised Edna I would take you into custody, but I never promised to send you back for trial. If you'll give me your word you won't try to run away from us, you may come along and help.''

"What would be the point of running away?" Helena said dejectedly. "I've got nowhere else to go." As the Duke let go of her head, she lowered it again to stare dismally at the floor.

Etienne d'Alembert gazed with tenderness and pity upon the young woman seated before him. As long as he'd known her she'd always shown excitement in life and a cheerful disposition through any adversity. It was heartbreaking to see her as she was now, a creature broken in mind and spirit. He made a silent vow that, if it were at all possible, he would prove her father's innocence and return to her the lost fortune and dignity that was rightfully hers.

Duke Etienne had cultivated, over many long years, the reputation for eccentricity. It was a common occurrence for him to alter the Circus' schedule without warning and take it to some other world altogether. Money was always refunded to disappointed ticketholders, and Etienne always made sure to present them with some token gift to make the disappointment more bearable. The Circus of the Galaxy was such a popular attraction that it was always welcomed to a new world, whether it had been expected there or not, and any bitterness caused by unexpected schedule changes never lasted long.

This eccentricity, of course, made a perfect cover for the Circus' secret activities on behalf of SOTE, and now it served a more private purpose. The day after Helena's arrival the Circus announced it was ending its run on Evanoe prematurely and altering its schedule for a stay on the planet Durward. Both of those worlds were startled, as were others that had been tentatively on the schedule, but there was little they could do other than accept Duke Etienne's decision. No one wanted to alienate the mercurial circus manager, lest he punish them by withholding the Circus from them for longer periods.

The journey from Evanoe to Durward took several days, even at top speed. Helena traveled in the Duke's personal ship, and few members of the Circus troupe saw her. She mourned continuously, despite the best efforts of Etienne to cheer her up.

The job ahead of them was complicated by the fact that they were not going to Durward on official Service business. The Circus' connection with SOTE was so top secret that it didn't even have a codename. When it was given an assignment at a particular place, the local agents were told they'd be contacted, but identities were never revealed. No one had told the local SOTE office on Durward that the Circus people would contact them, so Etienne knew he and his people would have to work on their own, without official endorsement or assistance. It would be awkward gaining information and acting on it, but he'd worked under such handicaps before.

He did have a few personal contacts of his own that he'd developed many years ago. He'd been on Durward a couple of times in his official capacity; once, checking some fruitless leads to the whereabouts of Banion the Bastard, and a second time tracing an unrelated case of a doctor who'd been performing plastic surgery on criminals to alter their appearances. That last case had been twenty years ago, and apart from routine Circus appearances he'd never worked on Durward again. His contacts could be dead or otherwise out of circulation, for all he knew. But he'd have to make the effort.

After landing on Durward, there was nearly a full day wasted while he supervised the very necessary tasks of setting up the Circus, arranging for publicity, and the thousands of minute details that were part of his job as manager. Even so, his mind was not idle. Even after several weeks, the planet was abuzz with speculation on the disappearance of the planetary Police Commissioner, Elsa Helmund. Etienne read himself to sleep over the news reports that had been published locally, and he insisted that Helena read them, too—not only to keep her mind occupied, but to encourage her to start thinking of new possibilities. She had, after all, been trained by her father, and Duke Etienne had a high opinion of both the teacher and the raw material he'd worked with.

Now that something was actually being done, Helena started coming out of her shell. As Etienne had hoped, she was too vibrant a person to remain closed off forever.

After making a few fruitless vidicom calls, he did find one of his old connections, a former high police official, now retired. The man was willing to talk about Elsa Helmund, so Etienne paid him a visit, bringing Helena along with him.

The informant did not have much more information about Elsa Helmund than could be gleaned from the newsrolls, but he did know a little more about the woman's personal habits. There were certain clubs and social circles she frequented, certain people she regularly associated with. Working on the theory that some of these associates might be connected with the conspiracy—or at least might know more about the Police Commissioner's current whereabouts—Etienne decided these leads should be tracked down.

The job was parceled out among several of his people,

including Helena. They did not want to scare away any potential leads, so all they did was quietly follow Helmund's friends to see where they went and who they contacted. It was boring but tricky detail work, and most of it would end up being totally useless—but a good agent knew that dedication to the minor tasks often led to data that could crack a case wide open.

Helena had been working for three days following one particular contact when she noticed something peculiar: She was being followed herself. At first it was nothing more than an uncomfortable feeling; she would look around and everything appeared normal, so she tried to dismiss it. But the feeling came more and more frequently—the feeling that someone's eyes were focused on her. Helena had been thoroughly trained in the art, not only of following someone else, but of what to do when being followed herself. She tried several subtle tricks in order to catch the follower in an error while not making it look deliberate, so he wouldn't know she was trying to spot him. Whoever was tailing her, though, was as adept as she was; she never caught more than a glimpse of him out of the corner of her eye, never saw enough to make an identification possible. She made sure she lost him, though, before returning to the Circus.

When she told Duke Etienne about the watcher, the circus manager gave a predatory smile. "We may be getting close to something," he said. "Somebody obviously spotted you. It probably wasn't the person you were watching—I'm sure you're too well trained for that—but someone else may have noticed you and wanted to find out what you were up to. That means they're afraid you might learn something. I think we should find out just who has been after you, and maybe bring him in for a little talk."

The next day, Helena went out to tail her quarry as usual, and spent most of the day in this trivial occupation.

It was not long before she again felt the presence of her own watcher in the corners, but made no attempt to shake him or look around for him. It was not until late in the evening that she made her move.

The man she was following walked down the street to the club he generally visited each week. Helena suddenly broke away from her pursuit of him and raced down an alley to the side. She hoped for one of two things—either that her own follower would be startled and break his pattern to chase after her, or else that she'd be able to circle quickly around and catch him from another angle, where he'd be more visible.

She ran quickly around the block, panting but excited at the prospect of some action. Her shadow was still nowhere in sight as she returned to the street she'd left so abruptly, and she was feeling disappointed when she heard the sound of a scuffle in the shadows beside one building.

Duke Etienne had not sent her out alone today; instead, she'd been accompanied, discreetly, by the Duke's niece, Luise deForrest, one of the Circus' top clowns and a superb agent in her own right. Luise had been sent to watch Helena—and, more important, to watch for anyone else watching her. Helena's quick break had been designed to lure the watcher out of his pattern so that either Luise or Helena could nab him.

From the sound of it as she approached, Helena could tell there was quite a struggle going on. Etienne had not wanted to send more than one person to help her; for one thing, too many people would make themselves more obvious—and for another, the family pride refused to admit it might take more than one d'Alembert to handle so simple a situation. Luise, her long black hair tied back in a neat braid to be out of her way, was locked in hand-to-hand combat with a man who seemed to be almost her match. Helena pulled out the ministunner Duke Etienne had given her, but although she was a crack shot, the two bodies were so fiercely interlocked it would have been difficult to hit her target. Instead, she launched into the fight herself, and with her help Luise was able to get a firm grip on their antagonist. The female clown swung her opponent hard against the wall, knocking the breath from his body. The man slumped to the ground, momentarily incapaciated, and Luise moved in for the knockout blow.

The man's body was sprawled in a patch of light that filtered in from the street, and for the first time Helena got a clear look at his face. "No, stop!" she cried to Luise. With great difficulty, the Circus performer held up on the blow she'd been about to deliver.

"What's the matter?" Luise asked.

"I know that man," Helena replied. "That's Captain Fortier. He's on our side—sort of."

9
Battlestation G-6

The d'Alemberts and the Bavols were not precisely sure what one of the conspiracy's "battlestations" might be, but the title did not sound promising. It conjured up images of heavy fortifications and impressive firepower. More than merely a battleship, it would not be designed to outrun or contact the enemy. Instead, it sounded like a defensive position where the conspiracy was prepared to dig in and fight back against almost anything the Empire chose to throw against it.

"We could call in the Navy and batter it into submission. . . ." Jules began hesitantly.

"But you don't like to be that heavyhanded," Yvette finished the sentence for him.

Jules grinned sheepishly. "Well, there _is_ something to be said for subtlety."

"There's only one person in the Galaxy less subtle than you, _mon cher frère,_ and that's my own dear husband. Nevertheless, you're right. If we call in an entire fleet to take care of one station, we'll put the station out of commission and learn nothing further. Sometimes a can opener is better than a sledgehammer.''

"Then, too," Yvonne pointed out, "we know the conspiracy is able to monitor our internal affairs somehow. If we put in a call for help, they might get wind of it and run away before we can catch them. Right now the only people we can trust are ourselves. I think we ought to wrap this up ourselves, and use the Navy only as a backup if something goes wrong.''

They spent the rest of the day thrashing out the details of a plan. They could not be too specific because they didn't know precisely what sort of threat they'd be facing; a lot of it would have to be invented as they went along.

For that reason, it was decided that Jules and Yvette would make the actual assault on the battlestation. They were the most experienced of the group, having worked together for many years both as agents in the field and as acrobats in the Circus. They knew every move and reflex the other had. And truth to tell, as much as they loved their respective spouses, they were glad to have a chance to work with each other again.

As agreed, Vonnie would stay behind and guard their prisoners. She didn't like receiving what she regarded as preferential treatment because of her condition, but even she had to admit her job would be vital. Not only did she have to keep their captives incommunicado long enough for the others to do their jobs, but there had to be someone left behind to notify the Navy if their plan failed. It was decided she would give the others two days; if she hadn't heard from them by the end of that time, she would call in reinforcements.

That left Pias in need of something to do. He agreed to pilot the ship towards the battlestation. This would not be as simple as task as it sounded, because he was almost certain to come under fire the moment he approached the object. His newly-acquired skills as a pilot would be put to the most severe test as he tried to accomplish his goals while dodging enemy blaster beams at the same time. It was a necessary task, but not one he was looking forward to.

The three SOTE agents were in full space battle armor as their ship dropped out of subspace near the coordinates of the battlestation. The armor was uncomfortable, but the alternatives to wearing it were even more so. If their vessel were destroyed, the armor gave them a chance to survive and carry on their mission.

They made sure to materialize well out of weapons range, so they could have a look at the enemy before moving in. At this distance, several hundred kilometers away, there were few details visible even through a powerful scope. The station was a large black ball of metal several hundred meters in diameter. Its surface bristled with projections that threatened anyone approaching its sights. It was difficult to tell, but it seemed to have its own engines mounted on the rear, making it somewhat mobile— although the agents doubted it was capable of any great speed.

"Can't tell much about it from here," Jules said regretfully. "We'll have to move in closer to see anything specific."

"If we get much closer you'll have to look pretty fast," Pias said, "because I'll be busy dodging blaster beams."

"There's no other way, I'm afraid," Yvette said. "We'll have to get close to it sometime, and the sooner the better; Boros can see us on her screens right now just as clearly as we can see her. The less time we give her to prepare for our arrival, the more chance we'll have to succeed."

With no further prompting, Pias began the ship on its

course toward the unknown opponent. He started moving slowly, building up speed at a gradual pace until he was zipping along a confusing path at cruising rate. This ship was not *La Comète Cuivré*, the fast little craft that belonged exclusively to Jules and Yvette; because the four agents had needed more than a two-seater to get from DesPlaines to Floreata, they'd taken *Le Lapin* from the d'Alembert hangar. Nevertheless, it handled with superb precision, obeying Pias's split second commands.

The battlestation grew larger in the scope, but it remained ominously silent. It issued no radio or subcom challenge, made no attempt to communicate with the tinier vessel. The blaster turrets swiveled to cover the ship as it moved, but there was no other indication of life within the somber fortress.

Except for the projecting turrets, the outer hull of the battlestation appeared completely smooth. There were no docking facilities, no viewpoints, nothing but barren metal. Jules, who had his eye on the scope, mentioned this to his companions and added, "It looks like they're not eager for visitors. I'm not sure there's any way to get inside. . . . Wait, there's a small ship docked there. It fits in so snugly it looks like part of the hull. It can't be more than a one- or two-seater. Unless it's used as a ferry, there can't be much of a crew inside. That's a break for us. And there, on that side—it looks like a small maintenance hatch. Again, not very big, but. . . ."

At that point he was jolted away from his calm reflections. The battlestation, deciding this intruding vessel had come close enough, began firing its lesser guns, and Pias needed all the speed of his high-grav reflexes to maneuver *Le Lapin* out of the line of fire. From this point on, they would be caught in a deadly dance; one slight miscalculation and the ship would be gutted by the burning beam of the battlestation's blasters.

It was Pias's show for the moment; Jules and Yvette could only hang on tightly to their seats as their comrade guided the ship through the treacherous combat zone. "Better think of something fast," Pias said without taking his eyes off his screens for a second. "The longer I stick around here, the more chance I have of dodging too slowly one time, and that's all it takes."

"We have to get in there," Jules said. "If there is only a small crew, we stand a good chance of being able to take them ourselves."

"That maintenance hatch you mentioned sounds like the best bet," Yvette added. "*If* we can get to it."

"There are no docking facilities, and the station wouldn't give us time to dock even if there were," Jules said. "We'll have to be dropped off in passing. Do you think you can make a close swing to let us off?"

Pias gave him a tight grin. "I'll peel the paint off that station's hull. Just give me a couple of minutes to maneuver into the right position."

Jules and Yvette took that as their cue to leave the control room. It was difficult to move through a ship undergoing a constant series of abrupt accelerations; they had to take one cautious step at a time, keeping a firm grip on the walls, acceleration couches, and anything else in reach. Adding to the dilemma was the awkwardness of their heavy battle armor; even though they'd trained in its use for years until wearing it was a second nature, it made each movement a special challenge.

Slowly, the two DesPlainians traveled through the central axis of the ship to the airlock. Once inside and with the inner hatch closed behind them, they opened the outer hatch and faced the inky blackness of interstellar space. "What you'll have to do," Jules explained over his radio link to Pias, "is shoot us out of here like a rock from a sling. Let us know when you're making the closest approach and then pull up; we'll push ourselves out, and the forward momentum we get from the ship should hurl us right into the hull of the station.''

''*Khorosho*,'' Pias answered cheerily. ''Did you learn this from one of your relatives who's a human cannonball?''

''We don't have any acts like that in the Circus,'' Yvette said. ''We'll just have to improvise this one as we go along.''

It took some time before Pias, dodging maniacally through the increasingly deadly field of blaster beams, could maneuver *Le Lapin* into the proper position to make the needed charge at the station. Finally the moment came when he was prepared to make the move. ''Get ready,'' he told the others. Aiming the nose of his ship directly at the maintenance hatch, he raced toward the station's surface at top speed.

Blaster bolts streaked harmlessly through empty space around him as he held to a tight collision course. Some of the beams missed the surface of *Le Lapin* by a matter of meters, but Pias gritted his teeth and did not flinch. The range between his vessel and the station diminished at an ever increasing rate. His eyes were watching four gauges at once, and his hands remained rock steady on the controls. If he moved too soon, Jules and Yvette would be shot off into empty space instead of onto the skin of the battlestation; if he moved too late, he wouldn't be able to pull out and would crash into the side of the metal planetoid.

As the numbers on his readout screen dovetailed into the course he had mentally calculated, his hands moved quickly over the controls. ''Now!'' he shouted over the radio, simultaneously activating the auxiliary jets for a quick sidewards motion.

Just as he'd promised, he came close to scraping the paint from the battlestation's hull. If the station had been a smooth ball, his maneuver would have been precision perfect and he'd have veered off into space again with only the slightest of space between the enemy fortress and his own craft.

Unfortunately, the battlestation was not a perfectly smooth ball. The constantly rotating blaster turrets were an uncalculable factor in the topography of the surface. Just as the ship veered off, one of the nearby turrets swung directly into its path. The tip of the barrel just grazed the ship, but at the high speed Pias was traveling, that was a disaster. The vessel shook with a major jolt that nearly knocked Pias from his acceleration couch, and it began tumbling uncontrollably on its course outward from the battlestation. Pias grabbed at the controls and frantically tried to stabilize the craft once more, but that took his attention away from the very necessary task of dodging the blaster beams.

One of those blasters finally caught up with him. Because of the ship's wild spinning, the beam did not catch it dead center, but sliced through a portion of the tail. As the high-energy ray hit the motor and drive components—already overcharged themselves through their rigorous action—the back end of the craft exploded, leaving *Le Lapin* a dead lump of twisted metal careening madly in an eccentric orbit around the battlestation that had destroyed it.

Jules and Yvette did not see the fate of their ship, so busy were they with their own assault. At Pias's command, they leaped out of the hatch, pushing off just as *Le Lapin* veered away from its headlong flight into the side of the station. They were now being flung at high speed directly at the wall. The spacing of this stunt was critical.

As it was, Pias had undershot the distance just a bit. The instant they left the ship's hatch they began firing their airjets to decelerate, and still the station was coming up at them much too fast. They had to wait until the last possible second to get the most advantage out of their jets; then, in one fluid motion, they twisted their bodies around so that their legs were under them, ready to absorb the impact like coiled springs.

As superbly trained acrobats from a high-gravity world, they were used to hard impacts, and the collision with the hull of the battlestation seemed little worse than the leap to the ground that had been the climax of their trapeze act. Tucking their heads down as well as they could in the cumbersome armor, they rolled their bodies forward in somersaults upon landing to absorb the rest of their forward momentum. Their move was almost too good, bouncing them off into space again, but a small correctional blast from their jets brought them back to their desired location. They'd ended up on the battlestation's hull less than fifty meters from the maintenance hatch they'd been aiming for.

Using their jets once more, they skimmed quickly over the smooth surface, safely within the minimum range of the station's big guns, to the hatchway. The hatch itself was closed and locked, but Jules's high-powered blaster cut a way through the locking mechanism in under a minute. He and Yvette forced open the doorway, knowing there was a chance they might unseal the entire ship if the inner hatch was open. At this point, they didn't really care. They had plenty of air inside their armor, and they knew Tanya Boros would make sure she was safe no matter what. Everything else was irrelevant.

The inner airlock door was sealed as well, however, so the ship's interior remained intact. They resealed the outer hatch and equalized the air pressure within the airlock and the rest of the station. As the green light came on, indicating the airlock procedure was complete, the two agents stood back from the doorway, expecting trouble.

And trouble came in abundance. As one of the few

points of entry into the battlestation, that doorway had automatic defenses trained on it. The instant the airlock pressure was equalized, the hatch door sprang open and a series of blaster beams sprayed the airlock from the corridor outside. The total energy pouring into that tiny chamber lit it like a miniature sun.

If they hadn't been in the heaviest possible battle armor, Jules and Yvette would have been instantly fried. As it was, the high intensity of the blaster beams nearly blinded them, and would have cut through their armor in half a minute. The agents did not give it a chance.

Yvette was in the best position to act. Quickly picking a grenade from the side of her armor, she lobbed it forward through the open hatch. The explosion rocked the walls, and the influx of deadly beams ceased immediately. The DesPlainians peered out of the hatchway at a twisted pile of rubble that had been a stack of high-powered blasters aimed into the airlock doorway.

The interior of the battlestation was an enormous latticework, like a building still under construction. Beams and girders crisscrossed everywhere, bracing the interior walls in every direction against possible shocks from outside bombardment. In the center of the sphere, the metal beams clustered more tightly together, forming a fortress within a fortress. The central sphere was obviously where the living quarters and control areas of this battlestation were located, and it was there the two SOTE agents would have to make their way.

There was no gravity within the station; everything was left in the eerie freefall of space. Jules and Yvette did not simply push off and go flying inward towards the center, however; if an ultragrav system were turned on while they were floating in midair, they would suddenly go crashing in whatever direction was "down."

Instead, they activated the electromagnetic soles of their

armored boots and provided their own clinging force. The magnetic attraction to the bulkhead was enough to keep them from drifting aimlessly, but not too much to rivet them to the spot. Cautiously, holding on carefully to the girders, they began climbing their way through the tangled web of steel beams and cables toward the heart of the battlestation.

The air suddenly erupted with sizzling heat as more blasters, mounted in hidden locations all around them, began firing. The DesPlainians fired back quickly. Their armor gave them some protection; they could afford to take their time to locate the source of the different beams and put each one out of commission. But even their plating was being severely tested by the repeated high-energy barrages.

The interior defense of this battlestation seemed no less thorough than the exterior. It had been designed to withstand assaults, and Jules and Yvette were still fighting an uphill struggle. Only their DesPlainian strength and reflexes, which enabled them to move faster in space armor than ordinary people, had kept them from tragedy, and it was by no means certain that this state of affairs could continue.

As yet they had not seen another living creature within this station. All its mechanisms, all its defenses, were operating automatically with the speed of a computer. The computer could not be frightened, could not panic, could not overreact or make a tactical blunder that wasn't programmed into it. The battlestation was a masterpiece of engineering, and the SOTE team was beginning to realize they might have underestimated it. They would have preferred to fight an army of living opponents rather than the cold, mechanical precision of this automated destructive device.

Just as Yvette blasted back at the final attacking beam, a new threat appeared. From an unseen launcher on the far side of the battlestation, a small but deadly heat grenade came lofting through the air toward their position. Jules's sharp eyes spotted the projectile coming, and he shouted an immediate warning cry of "Rube!" to his sister.

To someone trained in the Circus as they both were, that traditional warning of danger—shortened over the centuries from "Hey, Rube!"—brought an instantaneous response. Yvette looked around immediately and spotted the projectile. If the two of them waited here, the concussion from the grenade's explosion would at least knock them unconscious if the blast didn't kill them outright. And they would not be able to run fast enough along the girders in their magnetic boots to escape the effects of the grenade.

There was only one alternative. Jules and Yvette leaped off the support of the steel beams into the freefall of midair, hoping to propel themselves far enough away from the target area before the grenade could go off.

While they were in midair, disaster struck. Their fear that ultragrav would be used as a weapon against them proved justified. If the battlestation had been defended by a live army, the tactic could not have been used because it would have incapacited the defenders as well as the attackers. But the machinery aboard the station didn't much care whether there was a gravity field or not.

The instant the SOTE agents were unsupported in midair, the ultragrav snapped on. Instantly there was a "down" direction, and their free-floating bodies began hurtling toward the "floor" fifteen meters below them. The field strength was five gees, more even than they were comfortably used to, and the armor made them that much more awkward. Jules and Yvette grabbed frantically for handholds on the girders as they went plummeting down, but they could get no grip. The pull of the ultragrav was too strong, and even DesPlainians had limits on the speeds with which they could react.

The two bodies crashed heavily against the down side of

the station's outer wall. Although the padding within their armor absorbed much of the blow, the shock was still too great for their systems to handle easily. The agents were knocked unconscious and lay pinioned under the crushing weight of their own bodies and armor.

Safe and snug in the center of her mechanical spider-web, Tanya Boros grinned. Although the last report she'd gotten had said that Agents Wombat and Periwinkle had been captured, she had little doubt that this assault on her station had been made by them. Even though the attack had been totally unexpected, the battlestation had reacted as it had been designed to react. Lady A would be pleased that this latest addition to her arsenal functioned perfectly.

And in the meantime, Tanya Boros would have the excitement of conducting an interrogation personally. She had a lot of scores to settle with Agent Wombat.

10
_____ New Ally, Old Adversary _____

Helena and her comrade from the Circus, Luise deForrest, faced a dilemma: What should they do with the captured Captain Fortier? They couldn't let him go, but at the same time they didn't want to breach the Circus' cover by bringing him back there. Even though Fortier's loyalty to the Empire was unquestioned, it was bad policy to let too many people know of the Circus' connection with SOTE.

Helena thought of a compromise. She checked into a small hotel and Luise brought Fortier up to the room via the back entrance. From there they placed a call to Duke Etienne explaining the situation, and he agreed to come at once to find out more details.

While waiting for the Duke to arrive, Helena had more chance to converse with the prisoner. She wanted very much to hate him because of what had happened to her father, but found she could not. For one thing, she knew the captain was honest, intelligent, and doing his duty to the Empire as he understood it. Helena had to admit that if she'd been the one to discover the evidence against her father, she might very well have turned him in herself.

More important, Helena thought Paul Fortier a very attractive man. He was short and muscular, with a handsome face, dark hair, brown eyes, and a pencil-thin mustache. She remembered reading his personnel dossier after the Coronation Day Incursion; while his family was of DesPlainian origin, the last few generations had lived on one-gee worlds and so did not have quite the strength or reflexes of the true DesPlainians. She also remembered he was single—a fact she'd noted at the time, and which now popped into her memory with disturbing ease. Watching him lying on the bed across the room from her, she suddenly found herself thinking very unprofessional thoughts.

Angry with herself, she pushed those thoughts from her mind to concentrate on the business at hand. "Why did you come here, Captain?" she asked in as neutral a tone as she could muster.

"I should think that would be obvious," he replied just as coolly. "I wanted to take you back."

"But you've been following me for two days. Why didn't you just grab me and pull me in?"

"I wanted to see if you'd lead me to anyone else."

Helena stood up and wandered around the room, deliberately turning her back on him. Luise was keeping watch to make sure he made no sudden moves, but she stayed discreetly out of the conversation.

"Despite what you think," Helena said after a moment, "I'm not a traitor. The only reason I escaped was to find some friends and clear my father's name. I know he was innocent."

"If he was, no one is sorrier about his death than I am," Fortier said quietly.

"You're just saying that because I have you here at gunpoint."

"It's the truth. You and your friend could have killed me there on the street when you had the chance, but you didn't; I have to think that speaks of good intentions. You could have killed several of my officers while you were escaping from the *Anna Liebling*, but you didn't do that either. Your behavior isn't what I'd expect from a deadly enemy of the Empire."

Helena's fists were tightly clenched. "Nevertheless, my father is dead."

Fortier paused and took a deep breath. "That's not my doing. After you escaped, I reported back to Luna Base and was told to bring your father to Earth for interrogation. I handed him over and that's the last I saw of him. I was ordered to try to track you down, so I came here. It occurred to me you might want to check out my story for yourself, and this was the natural place to do it. I heard about your father's execution in the newsrolls, the same as everyone else. It was the Empress who decided he should die; you'll have to blame her for that."

It didn't soothe Helena to realize that Fortier was absolutely right. Edna Stanley held the ultimate authority in that matter, and the execution could not have taken place without her express consent. Sometime in the future, if—no, *when*—her innocence was re-established, Helena knew she'd have to confront her lifelong friend about the horrible murder of a good and loyal man. The prospect did not appeal to her.

The conversation was interrupted by the arrival of Duke Etienne. The Circus' manager had come disguised so Fortier couldn't recognize him; since Luise never made public appearances without heavy clown makeup, Fortier couldn't associate her face with the Circus either. The Circus' cover remained unbroken.

"Well, young man," Etienne said to the prisoner,

"you've made quite a name for yourself. I'm sorry we had to meet under such tragic circumstances."

"I didn't realize I was that famous," Fortier said.

"Your recent exploits have been justly renowned in certain official circles," the Duke told him, putting just enough emphasis in his voice to make his meaning unmistakable. "I even have a very personal reason to be immensely grateful to you—a reason which, for security's sake, I can't explain right now."

Indeed he did. Not only had Captain Fortier saved the Empire at the time of the Coronation Day incursion, he had also saved the life of the Duke's daughter Yvette. "Please accept my assurance," Etienne continued, "that you are among friends here."

"I'd find it easier to believe that if that lady didn't have her stunner pointed at me all the time," Fortier said dryly.

The Duke nodded at Luise. "Put the gun away," he said. "We don't need it anymore. Captain Fortier will remain with us of his own accord. I even suspect, when I tell him my little story, he'll volunteer to help us."

Fortier leaned forward on the bed. "You intrigue me, Gospodin. Please continue."

Etienne d'Alembert sat across from the naval officer, watching his face intently. "When Helena came to me for help, she told me your story of the investigation leading to her father's arrest. I have, in my time, performed services for the Empire along those same lines, and I respect your efforts. Nonetheless, something in what you'd said raised my suspicions—something you knew nothing about since it was well before your time. It was that something which brought me here to Durward."

"The unfinished business with Elsa Helmund?" Fortier ventured.

"Only peripherally. I suspect Elsa Helmund is an unimportant piece of the entire picture, merely a device to lure you from Lateesta to Preis. Something you reported *about* her, though, interested me greatly. You said you first became suspicious when you saw the necklace she was wearing: an integrated circuit chip on a golden chain.''

"Yes," Fortier said. "I'd been told that some members of a certain conspiracy wore such things as identification symbols."

"That was my information, too," Etienne agreed. "Have you heard of Duke Fyodor Paskoi of the planet Kolokov?"

Fortier searched his memory. "I think . . . A couple of years ago, wasn't it? Something about treason. The planet reverted to the throne and a new Duke was appointed. I'm afraid I don't remember any of the details; I wasn't involved with it in any way."

"No reason why you should remember. I, however, was involved with it in a large way, as was the young lady who'd just been pointing her stunner at you. When I first met Duke Fyodor, he was wearing an identical chain around his own neck."

"I guess that stands to reason."

"Much more to the point," the Duke went on, "I thought at the time that I'd seen such a necklace before, but I couldn't remember where or when. The memory did not come to me instantly and I quickly became embroiled with other matters, so I didn't worry about it again until the story of Elsa Helmund made me think of it. In the past few days I have thought about it quite a lot, and I've finally recaptured the elusive memory. I'd like to share it with you.

"Nearly twenty years ago I was performing some . . . shall we say investigative services for the good of the Empire. Certain traitors and other high-level criminals were being given new identities so they could escape detection. Along with forged identities, they were receiving plastic surgery to alter their appearance. I set out to discover who was doing these things.

"The trail led me to a surgeon named William Loxner, who had a practice right here on Durward. My investigation uncovered enough evidence to have him convicted for his crimes. I believe the sentence he received was ten years in prison. I don't know what's happened to him since then, although I intend to find out.

"I was telling you, though, about the memory of the necklaces. While gathering evidence, I visited Loxner as a prospective patient. My first sight of him was when he came out of his office, saying goodbye to an elderly woman and setting up another appointment for her. Loxner was in his sixties and the woman looked even older, easily in her seventies. I never saw her again; she apparently had no connection to the case I was working on.

"But I remember most clearly the fact that both Loxner and the old woman were wearing identical necklaces— integrated circuit chips on golden chains. Loxner was fingering his necklace nervously; in retrospect, I'm guessing that the woman may have been a superior in the organization. At the time, of course, the necklaces meant nothing to me, but I recall thinking how odd it was that two people would be wearing the same distinctive article of jewelry. Today I find it more than odd, I find it downright suspicious that such a coincidence should happen on Durward—a planet with such a scandalous past and now with a question mark for a present. Do you agree, Captain?"

Fortier's eyes were alight with the challenge of this puzzle; he was clearly as hooked on the mystery as the rest of them. "I'm not sure this business with the necklaces has anything to do with the case against Gospozha von Wilmenhorst's father," he said slowly. "But you're right, it's too coincidental to be ignored. Something more is happening here on Durward, and I'd like to know what it is as much as you would. Tracking down people after twenty years can be difficult. . . ."

"This is where I'm sure you'll be most helpful, Captain," the Duke smiled slyly. "You currently have the full cooperation of the police and other agencies, while I'm acting unofficially. You were very adept at tracking down tiny clues on the trail to Helena's father; I'm sure you'll prove no less skilled on this case."

Fortier's jaw tightened almost imperceptibly. "There's just one thing. Putting the gun away was a nice show of trust, but it was still meaningless since you outnumber me three to one. You've still offered me no credentials to prove I should cooperate with you, merely old tales and innuendos. I do want to investigate this Dr. Loxner, but how do I know it's for the best to share my data with you?"

"You couldn't stop me from doing my own investigation. I might still hold you here against your will, though I promised I wouldn't and I won't. My investigation will go more smoothly *with* your help, but it will get done one way or another. It seems more efficient for both of us to work together."

Fortier still looked doubtful. He had no firm proof that the other three still weren't members of the conspiracy trying to trick him into doing some work for them. The doubts and suspicions could have been argued for hours, so Helena took matters into her own hands.

"Trust must always be mutual, Captain," she said to Fortier. "Perhaps if we give you an indication of our trust in you, you'll give more to us in return. You came here to recapture me. I am willing, here and now, to surrender myself into your custody if you will help with this case. I'd like to work at your side, if I may; I'm not inexperienced at piecing puzzles like this together. But if you want you may put me under guard, handcuff me, do anything that will assure you I mean what I say. Does that add up to the right hour on your timepiece?''

Fortier stared deeply into Helena's face. He recognized the sacrifice she was prepared to make on behalf of this case. After all, her father had just been executed for treason and she could conceivably share that fate. She was literally putting her life in his hands.

But more than that, her final words sent a chill down his back. ''Timepiece'' was his undercover codename. For her to know it at all meant she must have some high connections in intelligence circles, with access to his dossier. His entire perception of her shifted immediately. Who *was* she, to be given such knowledge? It occurred to him for the first time that she might know far more about him than he knew about her.

''*Khorosho*,'' he said slowly, nodding, ''If you can trust me that much, I think I can risk trusting you. You have yourselves a deal, *tovarishchi*.''

The next morning Helena returned with Fortier to police headquarters. The Naval officer made no mention of her, no report to his superiors, nor did he insist on restricting her motions in any way. He did ask, when they were alone, how she knew his codename and she admitted she'd been given legal access to his files at one time. She would say nothing beyond that, however, and Fortier had to content himself with that tantalyzing piece of information. Helena found, though, that he was watching her more critically out of the corners of his eyes when he thought she wouldn't notice. His opinion of her was undergoing a thorough re-evaluation, and she didn't mind that a bit.

The first item they checked was the police file on Dr. Loxner. The surgeon had served seven years of his sentence in prison, where he'd been such a model prisoner he was released on parole. He adhered strictly to the conditions of the parole and, at the end of his appointed time, was freed from constraints. There was no record, at least on Durward, of his ever being in trouble with the law again.

They next checked with the Durward Medical Association and the Durward Board of Surgery. Dr. Loxner had kept up his membership in both organizations even while in prison, and had never been uncertified. Upon his release on parole, he was permitted to open a new practice in tandem with another doctor, and that practice had continued for another six years, until Dr. Loxner retired.

Helena stared at the file and went suddenly pale. Sensing her reaction, Fortier asked, "Is there something significant about that?"

The young woman pointed at the name of Loxner's partner. "Dr. Immanuel Rustin was personal physician to Duke Fyodor Paskoi of Kolokov. He specialized in prosthetic devices. He also worked as a member of the conspiracy, building robots. He built the robot that took your place a few months ago."

Fortier looked at her, his mouth slightly agape. "You know about that, too?"

"I know about a lot of things."

Fortier looked at her, not even bothering to disguise the admiration in his voice. "When I first met you, I naturally assumed you were the spoiled daughter of a Grand Duke. Since then you've been a constant source of astonishment. I keep wondering how much more I'll find out when I get to know you better."

Helena looked quickly away. She could not help noticing his use of the word "when" rather than "if." Her pulse was beating out a strange rhythm, and she felt safer changing the subject altogether. "I particularly know about those robots; they've caused a great deal of damage. This is a fascinating connection, because it ties Loxner in once more with the conspiracy, and with the robots. If he and Rustin worked on the robots together, he might have had some role in creating the robot of Herman Stanck.''

She suddenly grew very quiet, and Fortier wondered what she was thinking. She did not share her thoughts with him, but instead pressed the investigation even harder.

By the end of the day they had learned a few interesting facts. Dr. Loxner was reasonably well off, and had been able to retire to a private asteroid in the Durward system several years ago. There was no death certificate, so there was a good possibility he was still around—and still linked to the conspiracy. An attempt to locate his patient files, though, proved futile; the records had apparently been destroyed. A further check on Dr. Immanuel Rustin showed that the man had lived on Durward and had been a close colleague of Dr. Loxner for nearly thirty years, though they'd only officially been partners for the last six years of Loxner's practice. After Loxner retired, Rustin emigrated to Kolokov, where he took the job as permanent physician to Duke Fyodor. Helena had some idea of what he'd done from then until his death, when the Circus had investigated the Duke's activities.

The hotel room Helena had rented on the spur of the moment had been turned into the central rendezvous point so Fortier wouldn't learn about the Circus. Helena called the room and spoke with Luise, acting as liaison. They set up another meeting with Duke Etienne for later that evening.

Etienne and Luise were both fascinated to hear about Loxner's connection with Immanuel Rustin. It was Luise who had interrogated Rustin under nitrobarb and learned about the robots in the first place. She admitted to feeling a terrible sense of *deja vu*, as though the universe were closing itself together in a tight knot.

The Duke, too, could feel events rushing toward some conclusion. "I think," he said, "we ought to pay a visit to Dr. Loxner on his private asteroid. There are a few questions I'd like to ask him, and the answers might become very interesting indeed."

11
Turnabout

Despite the fact that it kept her perfectly safe, Tanya Boros was not happy aboard Battlestation G-6. She was a person who needed human contact about her, particularly masculine contact. By the very nature of this station, she was completely alone. No ship other than the one built to dock with it was allowed to approach unchallenged and despite the station's thoroughly planned defenses, she was unsure how well it could protect her in an emergency. To be on the safe side, she'd hidden a blaster of her own just inside the airlock of the mated ship. That personal touch made her feel much better.

Her only contacts with people were over the subcom: most often with the killers hired to lure Wombat and Periwinkle out into the open, occasionally with headquarters for her daily reports. Other than that she had nothing to do, and the boredom was driving her crazy.

She'd been excited to hear of Wombat's capture, and had actually enjoyed her short talk with him. Her great regret was that she'd be stuck in this damned station and never have the chance to repay him personally for having interfered in her affairs. By rights, she should be Empress now; her father was the oldest recognized child of Stanley Nine, and had been given a Patent of Royalty. Banion should have succeeded to the Imperial Throne when Stanley Nine was killed in a spaceship mishap.

Instead, her father had been forced to hide in shame and plot to recover what was rightfully his. Lady A had filled Boros in on exactly how large a role Agents Wombat and Periwinkle had played in the capture and execution of Banion, and in Boros's own exile to Gastonia. Tanya Boros was in a mood for revenge.

She'd been frightened by the unexpected assault, but the battlestation had worked precisely as it had been intended to. Now, to her great delight, she had Wombat, and an unknown woman who might well be Periwinkle, at her complete disposal.

The two SOTE agents were still alive and basically unharmed after their crashing fall. The machines had helped Boros peel them out of their battle armor down to the light jumpsuits they wore under it. They were now bound securely against the wall in the small chamber just across from the control room in the central core of the battlestation. Boros knew she should report instantly to headquarters to let Lady A know of the capture, but she postponed the call for a short while. Lady A would get them soon enough and could interrogate them to her heart's content. Boros intended to leave them alive, although they'd probably wish they were dead by the time she'd finished.

Boros watched her captives intently over the next several hours. Their short, muscular bodies showed they were from some high-grav planet, probably DesPlaines. The woman was not as strikingly beautiful as Boros herself, but still very attractive; it was the man, though, to whom she paid the most attention. She had an inordinate fondness for masculine anatomy, and he was a prime example. She noticed some recent bruises, possibly gotten from her own assassins. She made a mental note to discover what had happened to *them*, although they must have been eliminated in some way. In the meantime, Wombat and his superb masculinity were entirely at her mercy.

As the agents began to regain consciousness, Boros left them alone and turned, instead, to watching them on the internal monitors. There was always the chance they'd talk to one another when they thought they were alone and reveal something important.

Jules and Yvette came to and realized their predicament. They looked around, saw one another, and smiled wanly. They each asked how the other was feeling; aside from headaches, sore muscles, and major bruises they seemed in pretty fair shape. There didn't appear to be any breaks or sprains. Once the details of their health were established, though, they weren't interested in doing any more talking. After half an hour of silence, Boros turned off the monitors in disgust and went to see her captives personally.

"How good of you to drop by," she smiled sweetly at Jules, undoing the seam halfway down the front of his jumpsuit and baring his muscular chest. "I was beginning to think I wouldn't have the pleasure of your company this time around. And you must be Periwinkle," she added, turning to Yvette.

"What's a periwinkle?" Yvette asked innocently.

Boros shrugged. "Just a minor annoyance that will soon be eliminated. Nothing to worry about much longer."

The room lapsed into silence for a moment. Boros took the opportunity to run a finger down the front of Jules's chest. "I've dreamed of you, you know."

"Really? I'm flattered."

"Oh yes, Gospodin Wombat. You're naked in an arena,

surrounded by swifters and braknels and panna-cats. They're all very hungry and trained to leap at your particular scent. I play the scene in slow motion so I can watch every delicious moment. The claws rake their way down your body like so.''

Boros demonstrated with her own fingernails, digging them into Jules's flesh and ripping gashes so deep they drew blood. Jules made no sound; he merely watched Boros coolly, trying to size up what she would and would not do. ''You won't get any information by torturing us, I guarantee you,'' he said calmly.

Boros looked him straight in the eye and merely smiled. ''I don't want information,'' she said, chuckling deep in her throat. ''There are other people more skilled than I am who'll get *that* from you. As long as I leave you alive and able to talk, they'll be satisfied. I have my own interests in this matter.''

Yvette tried to divert the woman's attention away from her brother. ''That's fine with us,'' she said. ''The longer you delay, the more time you'll give our friends to return with reinforcements.''

''The ship that brought you here was blown apart right after dropping you off,'' Boros informed them. ''I don't think you should count on any help from them.''

Jules looked quickly over to his sister. Yvette's face was stiff with shock at the news of her husband's death. It was always possible, of course, that Boros was lying to see their reaction, but the calmness of the woman's tone made that seem unlikely. They still had Vonnie as the card up their sleeve, but that hardly comforted them in view of the fact that Pias was dead.

Boros could tell her little bombshell had had its desired effect on her captives. Her smile broadened. ''Oh good, I was wondering whether I'd ever be able to hurt you. This is going to be more fun than I expected.''

• • •

Pias found it hard to tell precisely when consciousness returned to him, surrounded as he was by the blackness of interstellar space. When his ship had blown apart, the explosion had knocked him unconscious and thrown him into the vacuum. Had he been clad in an ordinary space-suit, it would have been ripped to shreds and he'd have been asphyxiated; but the battle armor he'd worn held up to the shock. It contained its own oxygen supply good for many hours of breathing. Pias survived.

It took him several minutes to remember where he was and to realize the extent of his predicament. He was stranded in deep space with several hours of air and no transportation. Vonnie had been told to wait two days before sending in the Navy; even if they spotted a tiny armored figure the instant they arrived, he would have been long dead. No, he could not afford to wait for others to help him. He recalled the old proverb of his native Newforest, that a single deed was worth more than a thousand promises. He would have to act to save himself.

There was nothing immediately around him; the explosion had scattered debris all over. The only thing that could possibly help him was the battlestation, still floating leisurely in space fifty kilometers away. He wondered how successful Jules and Yvette had been in their assault. For all he knew, they might have taken over and were now in charge of the entire structure. But he couldn't afford to risk that assumption.

He didn't know how sensitive the detectors were aboard the station, so he had to proceed cautiously. If the screens could see him at all, he would register as just another piece of debris from the exploded ship—but if he started accel-erating too quickly, he would look decidedly suspicious. Slowly, then, he gave short bursts on the correctional jets built into his armor, pushing himself into an orbit that would slowly bring him near the battlestation.

After nearly three hours of drifting, he approached within easy range of the station. He could see the maintenance hatch where Jules and Yvette had forced their way in, so he knew they'd at least gotten that far. But there had to be another way in as well; having been invaded from that direction once, the battlestation's defenses would be looking for another assault there. Pias always preferred to do the unexpected.

His mind had not been idle while his body drifted, and he'd thought of another possible entryway. Floating around to the aft portion of the station, he came to the giant engines that propelled it through space. If Boros decided to move the station during the next half hour, Pias would be killed instantly—but if not, he should be able to worm his way through the exhaust tubes and past the nuclear propellants, into the body of the station itself. There was a chance of radiation poisoning from the ship's drive, but his armor should protect him from most of it—and the possibility of overexposure was a better risk than the certainty of asphyxiation if he did nothing.

The exhaust nozzle curved around him like an enormous metal bowl, blocking out the stars. He used the light on his helmet to scan the walls around him for the vents he knew must be there. At last he spotted them directly ahead. A vessel this size required a lot of reaction mass to start it moving, and the vents, while tiny in comparison to the size of the nozzle itself, were large enough to accommodate a man in space battle armor.

Pias wriggled his way into the vent and climbed slowly forward down the dark, narrow tube, lit only by his helmet lamp. He felt like a worm inching his way into the Galaxy's largest apple. He continued along until he came abruptly to the end of the line, the sealed entrance to the fuel storage tank.

He had his blaster with him but didn't want to use it; not knowing the nature of the fuel used aboard the station, he didn't want to set off the tank and suddenly be blown to pieces. Instead he studied the nature of the closed seal and decided to try brute force against it. The seal was designed to prevent the contents inside the tank from leaking out into the ducts; it had not been constructed to resist pressure coming from the other direction.

Bracing himself as best he could against the slippery inner surface of the exhaust tube, Pias pushed with all his strength against the flap. He could feel it starting to give, so he redoubled his efforts and was rewarded with a crack of an opening. He stuck his arm inside to wedge it open, just as a rush of fluid came escaping from the tank.

If the drive had been activated, pumps within the fuel tank would have sent the liquid out under tremendous pressure and Pias would have been knocked back out through the nozzle. As it was, the leak was a gentle stream in freefall, barely noticeable except that it covered his armor in a gooey mess and partially obscured his faceplate, making vision difficult.

With great difficulty he pulled himself through the small opening and into the tank. He was now completely surrounded by the liquid fuel and vision was impossible. Feeling his way slowly and carefully around the walls, he came to an external hatch. From what he'd recently learned about spaceships and how they worked, he knew a large vessel like this often had an engineer's entrance into the fuel tanks, to enable someone to check for leaks and malfunctions in the fuel pumps. He opened the hatch manually and slithered into a small airlock. When he closed the hatch behind him and activated the pump, the liquid fuel that had escaped into the lock with him was pumped back into the tank. In just a few minutes he stood in his armor, dripping wet but otherwise ready to enter the battlestation itself.

Pias pulled his heavy-duty blaster from the side compartment of his armor and held it at the ready. The inner door of the airlock slid open and he emerged into the body of the battlestation. Everything about him was quiet and still. He hoped his entrance had been undetected, but he could count on nothing. He'd spent several years traveling through the Galaxy as a gambler before he'd met the d'Alemberts, and he knew he was now playing one of the largest gambles of his life. Every defense of this station was geared to ward off violent attacks; he was betting it had little or no defense against a quiet infiltration like his. As long as he kept things peaceful, he would probably be safe. If fighting started, all bets were off.

As he left the engineering section, he found himself in a large, spherical cavern with crisscrossing girders. In the center of the spherical area was another sphere. If there were any people in the station at all, that's where they'd have to be.

Moving slowly and quietly, Pias made his way along the steel beams toward the central sphere. His head was constantly turning as he looked for any possible threats through his badly smudged faceplate. By moving his head slowly back and forth, he hoped his peripheral vision might spot any hostile motion that escaped his direct notice.

The stillness was ominous. He could never have guessed, just from his surroundings, that he was in the midst of a mighty engine of destruction. Nothing stirred, nothing moved but him. He could almost convince himself the station was deserted.

He reached the central sphere and found all the doors

locked tightly and, as part of the defensive nature of this station, there were no exterior palm plates to open the doors. Judging from how quiet things were, Pias didn't think the doors had been deliberately closed to exclude him; nevertheless, he now faced a decision. He could either wait here an indeterminate length of time until one of the sphere's occupants opened the doors in the normal course of events, or he could force the issue and blast his way in, upsetting the peace he'd striven for all this time.

Pias checked the tiny gauge in his helmet indicating how much good air he had left in his armor. The gauge read right on the empty line, meaning he had perhaps half an hour to breathe. So much for waiting.

The door appeared to be a thick sheet of magnisteel. His blaster could burn through it given a couple of minutes— but the instant his beam touched the metal of the door the alarm would be sounded, and he doubted he'd have any uninterrupted minutes after that. This would have to be a quick and dirty job.

Backing off a respectful distance, he braced himself against one of the naked girders and threw a contact grenade at the door. He waited until just before the grenade reached its target and launched himself after it, blaster drawn and ready.

The explosion rocked the battlestation with a shattering roar, blowing a hole in the door big enough for Pias to sail through easily, riding the concussion wave along the air currents. The automated defenses clicked on instantly at the explosion, but even the computer-guided weaponry had trouble at first deciding where to shoot. The blasters first trained on the doorway, sending their energy beams to a spot Pias had already passed beyond.

By the time the computer had adjusted its thinking to the situation, Pias was well into action. He threw a second grenade down the hallway ahead of him; the throwing motion slowed his forward progress and started him spinning, so he had to reach up against a nearby wall to steady himself. The grenade caused another teeth-jarring explosion and knocked out some of the automated blasters mounted on the walls—the blasters that were the battle-station's last line of defense against invasion.

More blasters fired at him from behind, but Pias's armor gave him time enough to turn and calmly shoot back at the offending weapons, knocking them out of commission before they could do sufficient damage to him.

Silence descended on the station once more—not the silence of peace, this time, but the heavy silence of an enemy contemplating its next move. Pias was sure he'd taken care of most of the blasters around him; the only other weapons he feared were bombs or grenades, and the enemy was not about to set such things off near its central command post. There would be too much destroyed in the process, and the station would be irreparably damaged while being "saved."

Pias had not thought about the use of ultragrav as a weapon, and the sudden gravitational field hit him hard. The five-gee force caught him unaware, but fortunately he didn't have far to fall to the "floor" of the corridor. The space armor absorbed a lot of the shock, and while Pias had the air knocked out of him, he was not unconscious.

His native world of Newforest had a gravitational field of two and half Earth gravities, and he'd been spending a lot of time lately on DesPlaines with its three-gee field. The space armor was exceedingly heavy, nearly doubling his normal body weight. He felt he was carrying a load four times his accustomed self—a burden that would stagger anyone.

Slowly, very slowly, Pias brought up first one leg, then

the other, until he was in a hands-and-knees position. *That's as far as I'm going to make it,* he thought. He gritted his teeth against the pain and crawled down the corridor. The lights suddenly went out, but he turned on his helmet lamp and continued the painful crawl.

There were a couple of doorways further down the hallway, both sealed closed. Pias took his last grenade and pushed it along the floor ahead of him. The grenade just reached the doorways as it exploded, shattering the metal doors inward. Pias then continued his crawl until he reached the doorways.

One of the rooms looked to be the control center of the station, but there was no one in it. In the other room, however, he struck paydirt. Jules and Yvette were bound and stretched up against the wall, sagging under the increased gravitational field. Tanya Boros was lying on the ground, barely conscious. She was not wearing heavy armor—but then, she was not used to five gees, either. By turning on the ultragrav within the central sphere, the battlestation's computer had immobilized her as well.

Boros looked at the hole in the door and the blaster in Pias's hand. She may have been a silly and vindictive woman, but she was enough of a realist to want to stay alive. "I surrender," she gasped feebly.

"Good," Pias said in a voice only barely stronger. His voice was carried to her by the armor's exterior speakers. "Now how do you turn this damned thing off?"

Boros gathered her strength together and said, "Peace mode" as loudly as she could. The computer, attuned to her voice, obeyed the command. The ultragrav shut off as quickly as it had come on, and the station reverted to freefall.

After pausing for a moment to gather his own strength, Pias pushed himself off the floor and floated over to

Yvette. He untied her and gave her the gun to hold on Boros while he quickly undid the helmet of his armor. The oxygen gauge read below empty.

"What took you so long?" his wife asked him lightly, though her concern was evident in her eyes.

Pias shrugged. "Oh, I just decided to take the scenic route."

12
The Talking Asteroid

The ship that approached Dr. Loxner's private asteroid was smaller than Captain Fortier would have liked. Knowing that Loxner was deeper into the conspiracy than had previously been suspected, he'd wanted to invade the hideaway with a full contingent of Imperial Marines. Fortier knew how well fortified a rock in space could be.

Duke Etienne talked him out of it. "We want information, not a war," he pointed out. "The Navy could pound that rock to pieces, but we won't learn anything more from that. If we go as unofficial individuals, Loxner will feel less threatened and we may get more out of him."

"But we'll be at his mercy," Fortier protested.

"You needn't worry about that," Etienne assured him. "I've got a few handy tricks of my own."

Etienne, Helena, and Fortier were the only people in the spaceship's cabin as it neared Loxner's private asteroid. As they came within fifty kilometers their radio crackled to life. "The asteroid you are approaching is private property.

Please change course to avoid trespassing, in accordance with Imperial Statue 6817.52.''

Etienne was prepared for that, and broadcast back, "This is a former patient of Dr. Loxner's, Gregori Ivanov. I must speak with Dr. Loxner about some surgery he performed on me twenty years ago."

There was a long silence at the other end before a response came back. "There is no record of any patient by that name."

"I, uh, didn't have this name when Dr. Loxner worked on me. It's been changed several times since then. It's inadvisable to broadcast my former name over an unsecured radio channel.

Another long pause. Then: "You are given permission to land. Please follow the beacon to the landing site."

Etienne acknowledged the command and did as requested, landing his ship in the small crater whose floor had been cleared for visitors to the asteroid. There was no other ship in sight, not even one for Dr. Loxner's own use. The trio wondered whether Loxner ever left his asteroid, or whether he simply had supplies brought in to him at intervals.

A long, thick metal tube snaked out of the crater wall and fastened itself to the small ship's airlock so the visitors could walk through the passenger tube into the heart of the asteroid without having to don their spacesuits. The far end of the tube led through a door to a small anteroom with plain walls and no furnishings. A camera mounted in an upper corner monitored the proceedings. The artificial gravity within the asteroid was set at a standard one gee.

"Permission was given only for Gregori Ivanov," a voice said through a speaker in front of them. "Who are the other two people?"

"This is my son Pavel and my daughter-in-law Lianna.

They go everywhere with me these days. I have no secrets from them. They are no security risks."

"You are carrying stun-pistols. They must be checked at the door. No weapons are allowed within the asteroid." An empty drawer extended itself from the wall on their left.

"Of course," Etienne said, quickly removing his gun from its holster. Fortier and Helena exchanged worried glances, but reluctantly followed the Duke's lead.

When they had put their guns in the proffered drawer, which then withdrew back into the wall, the voice spoke to them again. "Now that we are no longer broadcasting on an unsecured channel, you must state your previous name and the nature of your business."

"I'm sorry," Etienne said firmly. "I can only divulge that information to Dr. Loxner face to face."

"The doctor sees no one these days."

"He will see me," Etienne insisted. "I'm not here to seek a favor this time, but to return one. I have information vital to his continued safety. Certain security organizations know about his current activities. If he doesn't see me, I won't answer for the consequences."

Another pause from the voice, the longest yet. Finally, in measured tones, it said, "You may enter."

A door opened to their right and they found themselves walking down a long corridor carved from the naked asteroidal rock. The air was breathable but oddly stale, as though it had been sealed in a crypt away from any life. Their footsteps made dead echoes against the sterile walls. The silence here went beyond that of a tranquil retreat; it had a leaden, oppressive quality that bespoke moldering corpses. The overall feeling was not of someone's vacation home, but of a long unused mausoleum.

There were cameras all along the way to monitor their progress, and closed doors at intervals shutting them out of rooms that looked interesting. The dim lighting came from fluorescent panels on the ceiling. The light panels, the doors, and the cameras were the only indications of humanity in the lifeless hallway.

Etienne tried opening one of the doors along the way, but it was locked against his efforts. "Don't try to go where you're not invited," the voice warned them sternly. "You'll be told which rooms you may enter."

"Sorry," the Duke said. "I was just looking for the lavatory."

"Third door on the left," the voice said coldly. "From now on please make your wishes clear. You may not survive a second impropriety."

"Thank you." Etienne went to the indicated door and used the facilities provided because he didn't want to appear a liar. Not yet.

After the short interruption, he and his companions continued down the dead corridor until a door on their right slid open and they were instructed to enter the room beyond. They found themselves in a chamber, somewhat larger than the anteroom, with several badly upholstered armchairs scattered about the slate floor. The walls were a sterile white, bare of decoration. Little compromise had been made to human comforts; the room was hardly more hospitable than the anteroom they'd come through. It reminded Etienne of nothing so much as a poorly furnished doctor's waiting room.

"Please be seated," the voice said. The trio sat and waited.

A large triscreen lowered itself from one corner and lit up to present the three-dimensional image of Dr. Loxner. He was somewhat older than Etienne remembered him, a touch more gray in the beard and hair, a few more lines on the thin, wrinkled face, but it was definitely the same person. He still wore that identifying necklace about his neck.

"What is the important news you have for me?" he asked, looking at Etienne.

"I must see you in person."

The image smiled. "That's impossible."

"I only deal with men, not their images."

"In this case, *tovarishch*, I'm afraid you'll have to. My image is all that exists of me anymore. The corporeal form you knew as my body has long since rotted away. Only my mind survives."

Etienne d'Alembert wrinkled his brow. "I'm afraid I don't understand."

"Of course you don't. Few people ever would. A brilliant colleague, the late Dr. Immanuel Rustin, and I developed the procedures for scanning a brain and recreating its memory patterns in electronic form. The patterns of memories and synaptical connections is what makes up a person's mind. The memory pattern—the mind—can then be transferred and imposed on any other synaptical device, like a computer."

Etienne's eyes widened as the importance of what the doctor had said became clear to him. "You're talking about a form of immortality," he said in hushed tones.

"Thank you," the image said, smiling. "I always thought of it in those terms. It's nice to have it recognized by others."

"But this could be the biggest development since the discovery of subspace," Helena interrupted. "Why are you hiding it?"

"I published a few tentative reports discussing general principles. They were greeted with raging apathy. Not even vehement denials, mind you; I would have *welcomed* that. A good, hot controversy always sparks the greatest advances in medicine. But my colleagues weren't even that interested. I decided not to bother with them any further. I had what I needed; let them flounder about on their own.''

''You mean you've got the secret people have been seeking since the days of cavemen, and you've only applied it to yourself?'' Fortier asked unbelievingly.

''Oh, there was one other about twenty years ago. She appreciated what I could do. She had me build her an entire new body, physically perfect, superhumanly strong, and her mind was transferred into that. But she was a very special case indeed, a unique individual.''

''Where's the body you created for yourself?'' Etienne asked. ''Why can't I meet that?''

''Oh, you do think small, don't you?'' the image of Dr. Loxner laughed. ''Why should I confine my mind to a single, limited body when I can expand it to suit my whim? My friend thought the same way you do. I tried to tell her a computer would give her greater scope, but she said she already had a computer and she wanted a body for maneuverability. Personally, I think it was simple vanity, but who am I to judge her?''

''Who was this woman?'' Helena asked.

Dr. Loxner ignored her question. ''Instead of building myself a humanoid body, I built myself an entire world. My mind rests in a computer that runs everything around you. In a very real sense, I *am* this asteroid. I control the power, the lights, all the functions you've witnessed. So you see, you *are* talking to me face to face. I am everywhere you look. You are within me. I am all around you, holding you, controlling your environment. You can't escape me.''

The image chuckled playfully. ''Why else do you think I allowed you entrance so easily? Do you think I was really fooled by your excuses and lies? Do you think I wasn't told that people were asking questions about me back on Durward? Do you think I don't recognize Helena von Wilmenhorst? Because I'm not distracted by the needs of a physical body I have more time to consider the facts, not less. Because my mental patterns are part of a computer network, I think faster, not slower. I am immortal, I can't die. I don't fear puny creatures like you.''

''I see,'' said Duke Etienne calmly, rubbing his right thumb. ''Then perhaps you won't mind if we take the information you've given us and return to Durward.''

''I said I didn't fear you, *tovarishch*. I never said I was stupid. No, the three of you will never return to repeat what I've told you today. I control all access here, and I refuse to let you leave.''

To emphasize the point, the door to this waiting room slammed shut with a loud bang. Etienne refused to be upset. He didn't have to try the door to know it would be locked. ''I see, doctor. Do you intend to keep us prisoners here in this single room?''

''It might be interesting to watch you starve to death. I do have faster means at my disposal, however, if that proves too slow.''

It was Duke Etienne's turn to smile. ''I'm afraid you're a little too late for that, doctor. You see, you're not the only one among us who's a mixture of man and machine.''

''What do you mean?'' For the first time, there was an expression of doubt on the image's face.

In answer, the Duke held up his right hand. ''I lost my real hand in an altercation some years ago, and I replaced it with a better one. You know about prosthetics; I'm sure you can appreciate the workmanship that went into this. The thumb is a radio transmitter. Our entire conversation has been beamed back to my ship. The three of us didn't come alone; I had some friends hiding in the hold. I've just sent the signal to come in, so they should be joining us shortly.''

Dr. Loxner's image froze momentarily. From his sensors scattered about the asteroid, he learned quickly that Duke Etienne was telling the truth. Out of the ship's tiny hold swarmed a small army of Circus people led by Rick d'Alembert, the leader of the wrestlers, and Luise deForrest. They had been cramped in their narrow confines for several hours, and were eager for action. All were clad in heavy body armor; all were ready to face any menace the asteroid could offer. They did not come down the passenger tube from the ship, fearing it might be booby-trapped. Instead, they came out the emergency hatch and used power tools to work their way to the asteroid's interior, through auxiliary entrances used by the workmen who originally hollowed out the space rock.

"You'll pay for this," the image said coldly, and disappeared from the triscreen.

Fortier's sensitive nostrils caught the faint wisp of an unpleasantly sharp odor. "Hold your breath!" he yelled as warning, and pulled out his tunic to hold over his face as further protection against the poisonous gas seeping into the room.

Etienne d'Alembert turned and pointed his right forefinger at the locked door. From the fingertip came a beam of blaster fire, searing in its intensity. It burned through the locking mechanism of the door in a matter of seconds, and the trio lost no time escaping to the bare rock hallway beyond.

But there seemed to be no safety here, either. A fullfledged storm was raging through the corridor, a high piercing whistle accompanied by buffeting winds that blew them around. "What's happening?" Helena yelled, trying to make herself heard over the sound of the winds.

The Duke raced back toward the anteroom, and the others followed quickly. His voice sounded very far away as he said, "Loxner's letting all the air out of here. We have to get back to the ship before we die."

They raced to the anteroom at the end of the corridor, only to find the outside door sealed shut. The air was getting very thin now, and each breath was a fresh stab in the chest. There was never quite enough air to suck in, and it all wanted to go out much too fast.

"Stand back," the Duke said. "I'm going to blow that door—and if Loxner disconnected the passenger tube, there'll be vacuum beyond it. We can survive in vacuum for a very brief period of time. The airlock of our ship is perhaps a dozen meters away, and there's almost no gravity outside on the surface. As soon as you're out there, make a jump for the airlock. *Bon chance!*"

The Duke pushed them back a short distance from the doorway, unscrewed the middle finger of his right hand, and hurled it with all his strength at the sealed door. The hatch blew open with a shattering explosion, shaking the ground beneath them and filling the ever-thinning air with a thick cloud of dust and debris.

The trio in the hallway did not hesitate. The escaping air pulled the dust out into space, and they ran after it into the crater that served as the asteroid's landing field. The artificial gravity ended as they passed the threshold; in desperation they leaped toward the open airlock of their ship.

Etienne d'Alembert had said they could survive in vacuum, but he hadn't said that it would be pleasant. Almost immediately there was a pounding in Helena's ears and her eyes felt as though they were going to bulge beyond their sockets. Her upper lip felt wet and sticky as blood began to drip from her nose and bubble as it hit the vacuum. There was a shock of cold on her skin as her sweat evaporated into space.

As she sailed toward the ship she could tell she'd miscalculated her leap. She would hit the hull just below the bottom of the airlock and probably bounce back down to the ground. She tried to readjust her course, but there was nothing to push against; all she did was exert herself and use up more of her lungs' precious oxygen supply.

She cushioned her impact against the ship with her forearms and tried to grab the smooth surface so she wouldn't simply bounce directly back into space; that would mean death within a few minutes. She managed to let the hull absorb most of her momentum, but could not gain a complete grip. She slid slowly down the side of the ship toward the crater's floor.

She landed with a bump and tried hard to scramble to her feet. It was difficult to see now; everything seemed filtered through a red haze that she realized was blood, which had now begun bubbling through her tear ducts as well. Her eyeballs felt unbearably dry, and she kept blinking to moisten them; the liquid evaporated the instant she opened her eyelids again.

Her chest was burning with intense pain. She'd been unable to get a deep breath before running out into the vacuum, and of course there was nothing here to breathe. What air she'd had in her lungs was rapidly turning to carbon dioxide, but she knew if she exhaled it there'd be nothing else to take in again.

Her strength failed her and she fell to the ground again. Reality was becoming a painful red haze, cold outside and burning inside at one and the same time. She lay miserable on the rough ground, waiting for death to claim her and frustrated at the way her life was ending.

Then she felt a pair of strong hands grasping her under her arms and lifting her up. Through weakly fluttering eyelids she could make out the form of Captain Fortier, looking at least as horrible as she felt. Blood was bubbling out of his eyes, ears, nose, and mouth, and he, too, was blinking rapidly to keep his eyeballs moist. After lifting her upright, he gathered his strength and pushed her upward toward the airlock hatch once more. Helena floated up with agonizing slowness, her lungs threatening to burst with pain at any second.

As she reached the airlock level, Etienne d'Alembert reached out and grabbed her, pulling her into the chamber and holding her tight to preserve her body warmth. A moment later they were joined by Captain Fortier, who palmed the closing switch the instant he was past the threshold.

The outer hatch slid quickly shut and air began to pump rapidly into the crowded chamber with the most wonderful hissing sound Helena had ever heard in her life. She let out the very painful breath she'd been holding, gasping and gulping at the still-thin air in a desperate attempt to recharge her body after its horrible ordeal. Her companions were reacting the same way, and for a while the only activity in the crowded airlock was shivering and gasping for breath.

Helena's spasms of shivering brought her body floating into contact with Fortier, and the two young people clung to one another. As the shock of their exposure began to subside, they became more aware of their sensations, but they did not stop holding each other. They looked deeply into each other's blood-smeared faces, reading the other's soul and matching it to their own. Suddenly, realizing how ludicrous they looked, Helena began laughing. Fortier looked startled for a moment, then was caught up by the sound's infectiousness. Soon both young people were hugging each other tightly and overcome by a bout of hysterical laughter.

Etienne d'Alembert witnessed this bizarre behavior with an experienced eye. A wise, kindly smile warmed his face, but he made no comment. None was really needed.

A couple of hours later, when they were thoroughly recovered and cleaned up from their ordeal, the trio donned spacesuits and returned to the asteroid. The battle, if such it could be called, had long since been over. This asteroid had not been built for all-out defense, and the onslaught of armored d'Alemberts had quite overwhelmed it. The only injury on the invading side was when one of the wrestlers accidentally tripped over a piece of debris and knocked into another armored figure, breaking the second man's arm. Beyond that, the armor protected the d'Alembert forces from anything Loxner could throw at them.

Loxner himself had not fared so well. As the attackers breached one line of defense after another and approached the central computer where his mentality was stored, the former surgeon became desperate. He could not die in the conventional sense, but he had a great fear of being captured and interrogated by SOTE experts. As the armored invaders broke into the room, Dr. Loxner activated a special program, erasing all memory from his computer. A moment later, there was no trace of the man who claimed to have cheated death.

Although all official records vanished with the mind of Dr. Loxner, there was some physical evidence left behind. Several of the rooms within the asteriod turned out to be laboratories and workrooms where the doctor could continue manufacturing robots. His computer mind manipulated remote sensors, working with more precision than a human being ever could.

The main assembly room showed signs of recent activity. There were many pictures of Elsa Helmund and Herman Stanck in various poses. Some of the pictures were taken at recent events. These were clearly the images Loxner had used to construct duplicates of the late Police Commissioner and Sector Marshal. Fortier was particularly excited at this discovery.

"Some of the evidence I discovered in your father's computer," he told Helena when they returned to their ship, "indicated that he and Stanck had been working in the conspiracy for many years, so Stanck should have been a robot all that time. The evidence here is that both the Stanck and Helmund robots were built within the last few months. As far as I'm concerned, that's enough to throw the previous data into doubt. I don't know why, but it looks now as though someone went to great lengths to plant evidence framing your father."

"But it's all too late," Helena said weakly, shaking her head sadly from side to side.

"I never meant him any harm. I was just doing my job, trying to defend the Empire." Fortier held Helena's shoulders tightly and looked directly into her eyes. "Please," he whispered. "It's very important to me that you believe that."

"I . . . I do." Helena's voice was barely audible. She lowered her head and buried her face against his chest. "It's just so unfair, so . . . so. . . ."

Then the sobbing became uncontrollable, and Captain Paul Fortier stood holding and comforting her for the next hour and beyond.

13
Escape Ship

Tanya Boros was left weak and depressed by the sudden turnabout in her condition. It seemed that one moment she'd been in total command of the situation and the next she was a prisoner of the despised SOTE agents. Her soul was numb from the chill.

On top of that, she knew she was doomed. She'd been captured before as part of her father's treasonous plot and, because she'd played only a minor role in it, had merely been exiled to Gastonia. Her involvement this time was far more severe, and she faced only one possible sentence: death. Even if the Empress was uncharacteristically disposed to be merciful, the Service of the Empire would not forget Boros's role in the death of so many agents. Barring a major miracle, Boros knew her life was over.

She sat limply in a chair in the control room as the three agents crowded around her to begin their interrogation. "If you cooperate," Periwinkle told her, "we're prepared to be kinder to you than you would have been to us."

"What's the point?" Boros muttered. "I'm dead anyway. Why should I help you?"

"You may not have a choice," Periwinkle replied.
"We could always use nitrobarb to drag the information
out of you."

"If I don't have a choice, what does it matter? Go
ahead, use the nitrobarb."

The SOTE agents looked at one another. They really
wanted to avoid that if at all possible. If Boros died as a
result of the drug, they'd only have the one session of
questioning her. She knew enough about the conspiracy to
be worth more alive than dead.

"What if we promised you'll be allowed to live in
exchange for the information you've got?" Pias asked.

Boros gave a bitter laugh. "You're just field agents.
You can't promise anything of the sort."

Jules leaned over and held her head so she looked
straight into his eyes. "We can promise you a lot of pain
and certain death if you *don't* cooperate. We *may* be able
to save you if you do. Which is your choice: pain and
death, or a chance at life?"

Boros took a deep breath and let it out slowly. "It doesn't
matter how much clemency I'd get. You have no idea how
thoroughly we infiltrate the Empire. As soon as it's known
I talked, I'm as good as dead. They'd kill me as an
example to others. No matter how much protection you
gave me, they'd find some way to get to me."

"We wouldn't be so helpless if you gave us facts to
work with," Yvette pointed out. " A few names, some
places, and we're in business. You saw how thoroughly we
crushed your father's organization once we had several
leads to work with. If you give us something definite, we
can root them out before they get to you."

Boros closed her eyes and leaned back in her chair to
think. She rubbed at her temples with both hands, trying to

clear her thoughts. "Oh hell, what's the use of anything?" she sighed. "What'd she ever do for me, anyway, but stick me out on this godforsaken battlestation with only robots for company?"

"She?" Yvette said gently. "You mean Lady A?"

"Who else? She runs the whole damn show."

"What about C? Where does he fit in?"

Boros laughed. "There is no C. She did that just to confuse you. She told me she runs the whole thing herself, and just made it look like there was someone else to complicate things."

The SOTE agents glanced quickly at each other. If that were true, it would be a major revelation. "Who is Lady A?" Yvette continued.

"I don't know," Boros said with a shake of her head. "She doesn't take people into her confidence."

"What are her plans?" Yvette persisted.

"I don't know those either in any detail. She said she was waging a war on SOTE to get rid of the peskier elements. This operation was part of that, but I failed her. . . ."

Boros began to sniffle. "She said she was going to restore the proper order of things, that I was going to have a position worthy of my heritage. And then she sent me *here*, of all places. At least there were other people on Gastonia!"

Before Yvette could ask another question the subcom receiver came to life. A life-sized three-dimensional image of Lady A's head and shoulders appeared in the triscreen. "Time for your daily report, my d. . . . Oh, I see you have company."

Pias and Yvette backed quickly out of camera range, hoping their adversary wouldn't get a good look at their faces. She'd already seen Jules's face at very close quarters, so he was left to deal with her. "Good day, my lady," he said casually. "I trust you're not too happy to see me here."

"I am neither happy nor sad," Lady A replied calmly. "I am, however, disappointed. I expected better things of you, Tanya."

"She also told us there was no C," Jules said, just to see how the woman would react.

Lady A did not disappoint him. Her eyes lit up and she glared at Boros. "For that, you will die!" Then her face softened again. "Of course, you're all going to die. Each of the battlestations has a self-destruct device which can be activated from headquarters. It'll just be a few minutes while the commands are relayed. For your failure, Tanya, you must do the honorable thing and be destroyed with your station." The triscreen faded to gray as Lady A abruptly ended her transmission.

Boros sat in a stupor while the SOTE team was thinking furiously. "That small ferry ship nestled in the hull," Jules said, grabbing Boros by the shoulders. "How do we get to it?"

"It's only a one-seater," the woman said despondently.

"We'll be extra friendly," Jules said, "Quick, we haven't much time."

The thought of that little ship reminded Boros she'd stashed a blaster there in case of emergency. If she could get to it, she might still have a chance to save herself.

Jumping up quickly from her chair, she bounded out to the central hollow area which was in freefall and launched herself toward the spacecraft dock. The trio from SOTE followed quickly after her, not wanting to be left behind.

Boros reached the hatch first. Pulling herself inside, she made a quick grab for the blaster hidden near the doorway, pulled it out, and whipped it around to aim at her three pursuers. She fired quickly but her shot went wild, sizzling the empty air.

The SOTE agents instinctively grabbed at the girders for cover, and that diversion gave Boros just the time she needed. Closing the hatch door behind her, she went to the little ship's control room to escape from the battlestation.

Jules pounded a girder with frustration. "Damn! There's no other transportation away from here. Even if we got into spacesuits and left the station, we couldn't get far enough in just a few minutes to escape the flying debris. And if we did escape it, we wouldn't have enough air to last until Vonnie sends the Navy out here."

"Back to the bridge, then," Yvette said. "Maybe we can find the bomb and dismantle it. One of us should call Vonnie, too, before we explode, to tell her what we learned."

They returned quickly to the central control room, even as the battlestation shook with the departure of Boros's ferry. On a large screen they could watch the little craft's progress as it pulled away from the battlestation and began its flight for freedom.

They could not waste time just watching that, though. By unspoken agreement, it was Jules who went to the subcom set to place the final call to his wife. Yvette and Pias began frantically dismantling the control panels, looking for anything that might be interpreted as a bomb, even though they knew it was a hopeless cause.

A sudden flare on the exterior screen caught the corner of Pias's eye. He glanced up, froze for an instant, and stopped his frantic searching. "Look," he said quietly to his companions.

Where the little ferry ship had been was now just a bright light and an expanding cloud of gas and debris. The three agents stared at the screen uncomprehendingly for a moment, until understanding suddenly dawned in Jules's eyes. "The bomb was in the ship," he said in hushed tones. "Lady A knew how good we are at surviving, so she put the bomb in the one possible escape vehicle and chased us into it. She *ordered* Boros to stay here, where she'd be safe, thinking we'd try to save our own lives.''

"It very nearly worked," Pias said nervously. "Why didn't Boros go along with it?"

"She probably didn't know about the plan," Yvette said. "She told us Lady A never revealed anything she didn't have to know. Lady A was probably afraid we might torture Boros and get the information out of her if she knew, so she didn't tell her."

Jules nodded. "She was hoping Boros would blindly obey her order to stay and die on the battlestation—or perhaps she thought we'd selfishly leave Boros back here to die while we escaped ourselves. She didn't count on Boros taking independent action."

They watched the screen silently for a few more seconds until the cloud of wreckage had dissipated enough to vanish against the background of space. Then, more relaxed, Jules finished placing the subcom call to Vonnie, asking that she send a ship out to pick them up.

14
_____ Conversation with a Ghost _____

Etienne d'Alembert returned to Earth with Helena and
Captain Fortier. While the captain traveled on to Luna
Base to make his personal report to Naval Intelligence,
Helena requested and was granted a personal audience with
Empress Stanley Eleven. She admitted being very nervous
at the prospect of facing Edna under these circumstances,
so Duke Etienne agreed to serve as her escort.

The meeting took place in the same private conference
chamber at the Moscow Imperial Palace where Duke Mosi
Burr'uk had informed the Empress of the evidence against
Zander von Wilmenhorst. Helena sat nervously, fixing her
hair, checking her makeup, making sure her clothes were
straight—and at the same time wondering what she could
possibly say to the woman who'd had her father executed.

Edna Stanley entered the room without ceremony and
sat down at the head of the large oval table facing her two
visitors. A long, awkward pause followed. Both women
were about the same age, and had been raised together

almost as sisters. Now the actions and suspicions of the past few weeks had turned them into strangers.

Not knowing what to say immediately to Helena, Edna turned to Duke Etienne. "I suppose I should have you reprimanded for failing to turn Helena in when she first came to you." Her slight smile and warm tone of voice took the sting out of her words.

"I obeyed Your Majesty precisely," Etienne replied good-naturedly. "I took her immediately into my custody and I refused to take orders from her to go on a mission to clear her father's name. There were, however, no orders to return her to Earth immediately, and I have a standing assignment to investigate anything I view as suspicious. I merely used my instincts and discretion, as a good agent should."

"I hope I can always trust to your instincts and discretion," Edna nodded. That done, she turned to the heavy task of facing Helena. "I suppose you feel I owe you an apology for everything that's happened."

"The Empress need apologize for nothing," Helena said by rote, dry tears burning the corners of her eyes. "I just wish you'd had a little more faith in us."

"When you're personally responsible for hundreds of planets and trillions of lives, faith becomes a very expensive commodity," Edna sighed. "I had no choice but to do everything exactly as I did it."

"You could have called us, talked to us, let us explain," Helena said bitterly, looking away from her ruler's face. "You could have granted us that courtesy, at least."

"After your escape, I took a tremendous risk," Edna said slowly. "I had your father brought back to Earth and I had a private conversation with him. It was he who told me what I had to do."

Helena caught her breath, then let it out slowly. "Yes, that sounds like him. He *would* recommend his own execution if he thought it was the only way to restore your faith in the Service as a whole. He was completely dedicated to you—and you had to kill him to find that out!'' She could restrain herself no further, and burst into tears right in front of the Empress of the Empire of Earth.

Edna rose and walked slowly around the table to her friend's side. She placed her hands gently on Helena's shoulders and hugged her friend to her. ''Helena, dear, I'm sorry I forced you to undergo this torment. Knowing what this would do to you tore my heart in two. I know there's not a single thing I can do to make up for the pain, the sorrow, the agony I've caused you—but I hope I can at least do something that allows you to forgive me. Look.''

Helena lifted her head and gazed in the direction Edna indicated. Standing in the doorway was Zander von Wilmenhorst, smiling—the warm, knowing expression Helena had always loved.

The shock of seeing her father again was almost greater than the shock of learning he was dead. Helena sat stupefied for a moment, then sprang to her feet as though propelled by a rocket. She raced to her father and threw her arms around his tall body. She wept once more, but this time the tears were of pure joy.

Von Wilmenhorst held his daughter lovingly, stroking her hair and allowing the emotional release to flow out of her system. When her body was no longer racked with sobbing, he pulled away slightly and gazed into her eyes. ''Well, how do I look? Not bad for an old ghost, eh?''

From across the room, Etienne d'Alembert was flashing a smile that could have lit up a city. ''You're the most welcome specter I've ever seen, *mon ami*.''

''Oh, Father,'' Helena gasped between her tears. ''I thought I'd never see you again.''

The Head sighed and nodded. ''I know, that was the most regrettable part of this charade. That's why I sent you off to the Circus when I realized what I might need to do.''

"Sent me?" Helena pulled back, startled. "You did no such thing. You didn't want me to go anywhere."

"Saying 'no' is still the best way to manipulate children." Von Wilmenhorst smiled kindly. "And I made sure to mention the Circus prominently so they'd be in the front of your mind. I knew Etienne would take good care of you."

"But what was the point of all this?" Helena asked. "Why couldn't you have told us about it?"

Von Wilmenhorst cleared his throat. "It became clear to me as I listened to Fortier's story that the conspiracy had embarked on a massive and subtle campaign to destroy the Service's effectiveness, first with the attempt to lure Jules and Yvette into the open, then with the attack on my credibility. I received confirmation of this yesterday, by the way, when Jules and Yvette called in their report. The conspiracy had indeed declared war on SOTE according to Tanya Boros, now deceased. They also reported that, again according to Boros, there is no person named C, that the entire conspiracy is masterminded by our Lady A. I'm not sure whether to believe that or not; I'll tuck the datum away for further speculation.

"At any rate, I knew something had to be done to counter their attack. We'd already sent the d'Alembert-Bavol teams against the doubles, but we had to clear my name quickly or the entire Service would be suspect.

"I suggested to Edna that she announce I'd been executed for treason because I wanted to throw the conspiracy off balance. That would have been the one thing they wanted most, although they probably weren't expecting it. By giving them their fondest wish, I was hoping to draw them out and make them do something foolish to tip their hand. But it had to be done in absolute secrecy; I couldn't even let you two know the truth."

"Why not?" Helena said. "You can certainly trust Etienne, and you'd have spared me a lot of grief."

"But that, unfortunately, was part of the plan," Edna spoke from her end of the table. "You see, although I did have faith in you, I still didn't have proof. I had to see how you'd react. If you really were part of the conspiracy, knowing of your father's death would have spurred you to retaliate because you'd think the game was up. Instead, you kept working to clear him and passed the test with flying colors."

"Unfortunately, you were the only one to take the bait," the Head smiled ruefully. "Even after hearing I was dead, the conspiracy made no further threatening moves. That disappointed me in one respect, because I hoped they'd overcommit themselves in some way; but in another respect it's a hopeful sign. It shows they're afraid of acting too quickly on something that hasn't been a hundred percent confirmed. We must have hurt them more severely than we thought on Coronation Day, and they're being very conservative about what they do. For this reason, I don't intend to keep up the pretense of being dead any longer. We've already proved we won't be fooled by their discrediting tactics, and it would be too difficult to maintain the facade of my death, especially with as sophisticated a network as they have."

He escorted his daughter to a chair and sat down beside her, facing Etienne and Edna. "Well, that's my story. I understand you've had a few adventures of your own."

Etienne and Helena between them filled him in on their own findings. Grand Duke Zander went pale as he heard of his daughter's harrowing escape from the asteroid, but that expression was replaced by a cold smile as they told him what they'd learned from Dr. Loxner. "At last we're beginning to make some progress," he said.

"What do you mean?" Edna asked him.

"Twenty years ago, Etienne saw Dr. Loxner on Durward in company with an old woman who was wearing one of those identifying medallions around her neck. He says Loxner seemed afraid of her, as though she were a superior. Later, Dr. Loxner said he performed his mind transferral process on one other person, a woman, placing her mind within a perfect robot body. I don't think I need dwell too much on who that robot might have become."

"Lady A!" Edna exclaimed.

Duke Etienne took up the thread from there. "We have no direct proof, but I think we can make an educated guess about the woman's identity: Aimée Amorat, the Beast of Durward."

The two women were silent for a moment, allowing the thought to percolate in their minds. "Of course," Helena said slowly. "We never even thought of her before in connection with Lady A. We knew she'd have to be somewhere in her nineties by now if she was still alive, while Lady A looked to be a woman in her prime. But if her mind was transferred into a robot body, she could be any age at all."

"She was probably the old woman you saw twenty years ago," Edna said to Etienne. "She'd have been in her seventies then, probably desperate knowing she might die soon, ready to try anything to preserve her life."

"Loxner said she was vain," the Duke agreed. "That fits with everything we know about the Beast."

"Vain, cold, cunning, devious, utterly treacherous," the Head said. "We've managed, at last, to pin a name on our adversary, but I'm still not sure I'm happy about it. She's a woman whose beauty and intelligence snared an Emperor and beguiled an entire court. When that fell apart, she fled and managed to hide from the most thorough manhunt SOTE ever staged. She stayed hidden for over seventy years, and nearly managed to see her son installed on the throne. She's a skilled actress, and her ambition knows no bounds. She's one of the most formidable enemies we could face.''

''It just occurred to me,'' Helena said. ''On Gastonia, when she allowed Jules and Yvonne to inject her with nitrobarb, it might have been the real stuff. She'd have no reason to be afraid of it; it'll have no effect on her. Stunners will have no effect on her. In fact, there's damned little of anything she'd be afraid of except a bomb or a blaster.''

''This would also explain the preferential treatment she gave Tanya Boros—her granddaughter. And it makes what finally happened all the more ironic.'' He explained to Helena and Etienne the circumstances of Boros's death in the booby-trapped escape ship.

''Now that we know *who* we're dealing with,'' von Wilmenhorst continued, ''we can finally start making some plans of our own. The Service has a long background file on Aimée Amorat; while it's considerably out of date, it may give us a few things to work on. We can at least draw up a preliminary psychological profile to understand our enemy a little better.'' He lapsed into thought as he considered all the actions that needed to be taken.

''What intrigues me,'' Etienne said, ''is Loxner's mind transferral process. He developed a form of immortality, and now it's gone with him.''

''Not necessarily,'' Edna replied. ''That's one of the nice things about science—if a process is important enough it can always be recreated. I can authorize some Imperial research grants and steer cyberneticists toward those published papers Loxner mentioned. If there's anything there at all, the technique will be rediscovered.''

She paused to consider some of the implications. "If this works, it will revolutionize the entire Galaxy."

Etienne d'Alembert, meanwhile, cleared his throat and went to sit beside the Head. He whispered in von Wilmenhorst's ear for several minutes, and the Grand Duke's face broke into a wide grin. He looked back at his daughter.

"Duke Etienne tells me you've developed an attachment for our Captain Fortier," he said.

Helena blushed hotly. "Well, he saved my life," she admitted.

The Head's smile broadened. "Such bravery shouldn't go unrewarded," he said. "I've been trying to develop closer ties with Naval Intelligence for several months. It occurs to me that what we need is a senior officer from each branch to act as official liaison with the other. Would you mind the additional workload if you and Captain Fortier were assigned to coordinate our mutual activities?"

Helena's squeal of joy indicated she would not mind that in the least.